Return to:
Arizona Pioneers' Home
300 South McCormick Street
Prescott, Arizona 86303
928-445-2181

SKIVVY

Little Emily Skeffington started work as a 'tweeny' in the local 'great house' in the latter part of Victoria's reign. Vividly she tells of life below stairs; of her brutal seduction and of the birth of her son, whose fortunes she had perforce to follow thereafter at a distance. She describes her marriage, and widowhood; and her eventual refuge with her 'Monsieur', whom she loved devotedly.

This is Skivvy's story as she recalls it at the end of her days.

SKIVVY

Margery Lawrence

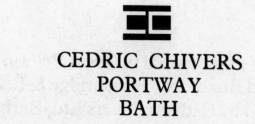

CEDRIC CHIVERS
PORTWAY
BATH

First published 1961
by
Robert Hale & Co. Ltd
This Large Print edition published by
Cedric Chivers Ltd
by arrangement with the copyright holder
at the request of
The London & Home Counties Branch
of
The Library Association
1976

678 Benntley 1200

ISBN 0 85997 166 X

This Book is Dedicated To
CYNTHIA LOCKHART-MUMMERY
With the Author's Love and Thanks
For her Long and Loyal Friendship

Photoset and Printed in Great Britain by
Redwood Burn Ltd, Trowbridge & Esher
Bound by Cedric Chivers Ltd, Bath

069721

CONTENTS

LT

PROLOGUE

by Sallie Stilwell

The following story came into existence in a
very odd way. I was staying with my husband's mother in the Dower House—people
still call it that, though Stilwell Manor is now
a school, and Evelyn and I live in a studio flat
in Chelsea, convenient for Eve's work as an
Announcer on ATV. She had gone to rest one
afternoon, and I, rather bored, was rooting
about the window-seat of the old study, trying
to see whether it would be possible to put in
central heating when the old lady died and we
took over the Dower House ourselves; that is,
if we have enough money to run a country
house in addition to the flat. We aren't at all
well-off nowadays, though once upon a time
the Stilwells were big landowners and very
rich. Now all my darling Eve is heir to is the
Manor House and the Dower House, and a
few acres of land which provide him with a
little rough shooting. He was out shooting
with some friends on this particular day.

There is a wide seat below the window in
the study, covered with a brown velvet pad. I

had imagined that there was only emptiness behind the panelled wooden front of the seat. But when I pulled off the velvet pad I saw that the wooden top below it was meant to be lifted up. The top was in three sections. The two short end ones were easy to lift, but the long centre section had been painted over so often that it wouldn't move at first. The paint had dried in the crannies. But my curiosity was aroused and I was not to be defeated by some old paint, so I found a chisel and dug away at the paint until I was able to lift up the lid.

Inside there was the usual litter of old stuff—croquet balls and mallets, some old tennis shoes, dusty old exercise books—the usual junk one finds in any hidey-hole in an old house. I was just going to shut down the lid, when in one corner I noticed a bundle of greyish material. I pulled it out and unrolled it and found that it was an old-fashioned dress—long skirt and high collar and buttons all down the front of the lined bodice. Inside the dress was a blue and white checked apron, and inside this again a big bundle of papers— old exercise books and a mass of loose sheets, all covered with closely-scribbled writing.

I was awfully intrigued. At first I thought I would show it to my mother-in-law. Then I decided that I had better not, as if I did, I'd have to admit that I had forced open the lid of the window-seat. She is a dear in many ways, but she's as touchy as the devil over having the tiniest alteration made at the Dower House. 'Leave it as it is, darling,' she'll say, 'while I am here. You can do what you like with it when I am gone.' So I closed the lid and put back the pad, and carried the papers up to my room and started to sort them out.

I had an idea, at first, that I might have found a cache of family archives, missing perhaps for centuries, but no such luck! The papers seemed to be a sort of diary, but it wasn't easy to piece them together, for the writer had scribbled on both sides of the sheets and hadn't always numbered them, either. Still, what I *could* read fascinated me, and when Eve came home and I told him what had happened and showed him the papers, he was as excited about them as I was.

We discussed them while we were changing for dinner, Eve's mother always insists that we shall change. Eve agreed with me that it would be best to keep the matter to ourselves, at any rate until we'd sorted out the papers and gone through them. Mercifully Mother always goes to bed early which lets us be alone most evenings. So, as soon as we had had coffee and she had said good night, we scuttled upstairs to our own room and started upon the job of sorting out the papers.

It was soon obvious that it would take us days before we could get the hang of what the MS was all about. All we could tell for certain in that first evening was that it was all in the same hand, in a rather uneducated hand-writing, with here and there a few spelling mistakes and slips in grammar, but on the whole not at all badly constructed. We sat before a blazing fire—I must say that, American as I am with a yen for central heating, there's a lot to be said for the look and feel of a real open fire—and read and sorted, and sorted and read. We read bits aloud to each other as we went along, bits of what was obviously an exciting story; and at last Eve put down his handful of papers and looked at me.

'Skivvy?' he said, slowly. 'Sallie, I believe I'm beginning to see daylight. It's a kind of life-story, written in diary form, and I believe I know who wrote it. There was an old woman living here in 1945, after the war ended. An old family servant. She did something rather heroic for Father in the war—I forget now exactly what it was, something to do with bombing and an air-raid shelter. She was called "Skivvy" I remember. I didn't know what it meant until Mother explained to me that "Skivvy" was a vulgar word that used to be used for a servant. Look, this page says that she was called "Skivvy". This story, whatever it is, must have been written by that old woman.'

CHAPTER ONE

I START OUT IN LIFE

MY NAME is Emily Skeffington, and I was born in the year 1875 on a farm in the village of Dorminster in Surrey. It seems to me, on looking back—for I'm an old woman now—that the summers when I was a child were always warm and sunny, the fruit in the orchard always ripe, and my grandmother, who brought me up, always kind. I know, of course, that that can't have been true, but it looks that way to me now, and certainly the farm was a pretty place and the life there just the sort to appeal to a child.

My grandfather had a mixed farm, cows, pigs, chickens, and so on, and a few acres given over to crops of various kinds. But it was the animals that chiefly appealed to me, and in my memory I seem continually to have been surrounded by hordes of these, from the baby chicks and ducklings which I adored, to the pigs which I did not. I was the only child on the farm, but I was never spoilt, for my grandmother saw to it that I wasn't. She'd 'done enough spoiling' of her daughter, my

1

mother, 'to last a lifetime and look at the result"! She would jerk this out with a spurt of bitterness that somehow struck me like a blow, so that something inside me seemed to curl up to hide from further hurt.

It was a long time before I knew the truth about my mother. She had been an only child, her parents' darling, the prettiest girl in the village, petted and spoilt. Then, when she was barely seventeen, along had come a handsome scamp of a commercial traveller, calling at the farm with his samples. He'd dallied with her, filled her silly head with tales of London, and the gay life they would lead there—the old tale with the old, old result. One day the silly girl was missing. She'd run away with him. She spent a few months with him in London—I suppose they were happy months. Then she discovered that he was married, and she came back to the farm carrying me—and died, poor lass, in giving me birth.

There was a frightful scandal, of course, and many criticised my grandmother for keeping me, instead of sending me to an orphanage. But my grandfather backed her up in her decision to keep and rear me herself, and after awhile the village accepted the situation. Farmer Skeffington and his wife were powerful figures in the locality, and it was as well to keep in with them, the owners of the biggest farm in Dorminster.

As far as I remember, there were fifteen or sixteen hands on the farm in those days, with a few outside workers at harvest time and for the fruit picking. The farm house itself was a big, rambling, old red-brick place, with a large garden and orchard around it. In one corner of the garden there were nothing but herbs, tansy, spearmint, basil and comfrey, and things like that. My grandmother, who was Scottish, was a great one for making simples, and she made such good ones that even ladies like Lady Stilwell from Stilwell Hall would drive over to buy them. I used to like the days when Lady Stilwell called, for she was a young and lovely lady, always most wonderfully dressed. She used to come in her elegant carriage, with the two prancing horses, and the footman sitting beside the coachman on the box, ready to jump down to open the carriage door for her. They were days to be marked with white stones in my memory, and when she brought, as she often did, her little girl with her, my cup of joy would be full.

Angela was about four years my junior, and as pale in colouring as I was bright. I was a chubby, red-cheeked child with curling dark

3

hair; she was small-boned, slender and fair, with blue eyes and light brown hair that fell below her waist. She and I used to play together while her mother got through her business with my grandmother, or, if it was fine enough, we would wander about the garden and round the milking sheds.

As far back as I can remember, my grandmother taught me to take my share in the work of the household. I learnt to cook and wash and iron, and to make and mend, first my dolly's clothes and then my own, and, of course, sweeping and dusting and polishing and doing all the other things that had to be done about a farmhouse. My grandmother was determined not to make with me the mistakes she had made with her own daughter, and nothing was ever allowed to interfere with the strict training she had planned. I was to learn all the practical household arts that a woman should know, and learn them so thoroughly that, in whatever situation I might find myself in later life, I should never be without the capacity to earn my living. Nor did she neglect my education in other respects. She taught me my letters herself, and how to add up and do simple sums, and when I had a fair grasp of all she could teach me, I was sent to the dame school in the village, a little school kept by a kindly old body who had been a governess in her youth and had better qualifications to teach than had most of the women who ran such schools at that time.

I did well at school, and when I was thirteen my grandmother called me to her one day, and told me that she was pleased with the progress I had made, and pleased, too, with the way I had profited by her training in household work. She said I was well-grown for my age, strong and healthy, and, she hoped, willing, and it was time I thought about going into service. She herself had been in service and had climbed from kitchenmaid to cook before she married my grandfather, and had never regretted it, and now she wished me to go into service, too. So she put on her Sunday dress and made me put on mine, and took me to see Mrs. Beck, the housekeeper at Stilwell Manor.

I was all agog with excitement when I heard where we were going, and I prayed hard that I might please Mrs. Beck and get taken on at the Manor. The idea of being near my lovely Lady Stilwell, and perhaps being allowed to wait upon her sometimes, went to my head. My grandfather drove us over in his dog-cart, my grandmother on the front seat beside him, and me behind, with a basket containing a dozen fresh eggs, a pound of butter, and a pint of thick cream in a sealed bottle; at my feet—presents for Mrs. Beck from the farm.

'Does no harm to grease folk's palms a bit at times,' my grandmother said, and there was no doubt that the gifts would make the initial steps of my path a little easier.

When at last we reached the Manor, I gaped at it in awe. It seemed to me an enormous place, though, in reality it was small compared with some of the veritable palaces owned by many wealthy families. A wave of fright swept over me, and if I hadn't been with my grandparents I think I should have turned tail and run away. But I had no chance to do that, and I sat dumb and shivering with nerves as the dog-cart turned into the stable-yard and my grandfather drew up.

A lanky lad with a freckled face and a shock of almost lint-white hair ran out and held the horse's head, and we all got down. The lad knew my grandfather, and pulled his forelock with a grin. My grandfather told him that we had come to see Mrs. Beck and that she would be expecting us, and Johnny—I found later that that was his name—pulled a big brass bell in a door that looked out from

6

the back of the mansion on to the stable yard. A neat little maid, capped and aproned, opened the door, and my grandmother sailed in with me trailing behind her, while grand-father went off to have a gossip with the head groom, who was an old friend of his.

Mrs. Beck was a lean, pale-faced woman, somewhere between fifty and sixty, with thin lips and sharply-watchful dark eyes. She came into the room into which we had been shown with a great rustling of skirts, and embraced my grandmother effusively, exclaiming over the eggs and butter and cream. She eyed me with a keen, appraising glance, as I muttered my greeting, that made me blush scarlet, and I sat down on the edge of the chair she indicated in an agony of shy-ness, which grew rather than diminished as she and my grandmother sat exchanging their news.

The little maid came in with tea, which she set out decorously and then retired. Just as she was closing the door, she put out her tongue at me, a gesture which startled and dismayed me, though I learnt the reason for it a few minutes later. Mrs. Beck was reading the letter my school teacher had given me to bring, and when she had read it, she folded it up and returned it to my grandmother.

7

'It's good enough as far as it goes,' she said. 'But I don't much care for a girl who's too good at book learning. Girls who can read are apt to have their noses in some silly book or other, reading all manner of nonsense instead of heeding their work. I want a good, steady, sensible girl who'll do as she's told and keep a civil tongue in her head. Not one that gives back answers like that little madam who brought in the tea. Pert as you please—always ready to scamp her work and idle and gossip with the other girls, or make eyes at the lads.'

She eyed me sharply.

'If I give you a chance here, Emily—and I might do it as I'm pressed for help with a houseful of guests and that girl leaving at the end of the week—and good riddance, too! If I give you her place as kitchenmaid, that's a thing you'll have to understand from the start. No fooling round with any of the men or out you'll go!'

'Addie Beck, there's no call for you to talk that way to my grand-daughter,' my grand-mother said sharply. 'She's been brought up right, as you'll find.'

'Ah, now, don't take offence,' Mrs. Beck said, her sharp voice suddenly oozing sweetness. 'We all know what you are and—and what your grand-daughter is likely to be.'

There was a short silence, and I realized that both women were eyeing each other like fencers with poised swords, ready to attack. Long afterwards when I knew my mother's story, which I did not then, I knew that words 'And what your daughter was' had trembled on the tip of the housekeeper's tongue, but she had not dared to utter the taunt at the look in my grandmother's eyes. My grandmother ended the silence with a curt:

'Then don't waste time warning Emily against something she's never likely to do!' And the tense atmosphere was dispelled and the two women resumed their chatting.

I was too nervous to do much justice to the sumptuous tea which had been provided, and when it was over and the interview finished with a 'Well, I'll think it over and let you know,' from Mrs. Beck, I followed my grandmother out to the yard feeling miserably that I had not been accepted. But my grandmother laughed at my gloomy face when I ventured to say as much.

'Oh, she'll take you,' she said. 'She was only too pleased at the chance of getting you. I could see that. She's wanting a girl to take the place of that silly young piece, and a grand-daughter of Farmer's Skeffington's far too

9

good to miss!'

'Then why didn't she say so?' I asked puzzled.

Grandfather chuckled as he touched up the horse with the whip to make him get along a little faster.

'That's Addie Beck all over,' he said. 'Making a great business of it all—pretending she's got to consult my lady before deciding, when she might just as well have said to-day that she'll take you.'

My grandparents were right. The next day a letter arrived from Mrs. Beck, written on grand thick white notepaper with a red coronet at the top of the sheet, to say that she would accept me for the post, and as the other girl had left without working out her week, she would be glad if I would go as soon as possible, and I would need such-and-such things in the way of clothes.

My grandmother frowned as she looked down the list.

'If Addie Beck thinks she can teach me what a girl wants who's going out to service, she can think again!' she said grimly. 'I've worked in families every bit as good as hers, and so I'll tell her if I get a chance. But all the same I won't have my grand-daughter go to her lacking a single thing—no, nor with

anything mended neither! We'll go into Dorminster tomorrow to buy material and get
Mrs. Nudd in to help us make what's
needed—and Addie can whistle for her new
kitchen-maid until next week.'

CHAPTER TWO

I COME TO STILWELL MANOR

IT WAS a fine Sunday in May when I set out for the Manor—not in the dog-cart this time. My grandmother said that the dog-cart was too fine for a kitchenmaid to arrive at her new place in, and Mrs. Beck would say I was putting on airs. So it was in the old farm cart, which was generally used for taking fruit or eggs to market, in which I set off on my great adventures.

I had put my hair up the day before. My dark, curly hair was scraped back from my round cheeks, and coiled in a rosette of plaits on the top of my head, the best way to do it, my grandmother said, for the pad of plaits would act as an anchorage for the cap that was to be my future daily wear. I wore a new dress of some olive-green material, buttoned up in front and high to the neck, and the generous outfit of clothes was packed into a straw holdall and a little black hair trunk, studded with brass nails, which had been my mother's, and which was now brought down from the attic and handed over to me with many warnings to take care of it.

It was with a good many tears that I said good-bye to the farm which had been my home and which I had never before left even for one night. My grandfather was so affected by my departure that he refused to drive me to the Manor himself, and deputed Ben, one of the farm hands, to take me. And my grandmother, who for days had been more irritable towards me than usual—due, though I did not realize it then, to her heartache at losing me—suddenly softened as the cart came to the door, and took me into her arms with an intensity of affection that surprised me.

'Good-bye, my girl,' she whispered. 'God be with 'ee. Work hard and say your prayers and you'll do all right. We'll be seeing you on your days off, and if aught goes wrong, why, you've always your home to come back to.'

The tears filled my eyes as we drove away, and I couldn't see the farm because of them. I cried for a good ten minutes—until I felt Ben's hand patting my knee.

'Now don't 'ee cry any more, my lass,' he said kindly. ''Tis 'ard to go out alone into the world for the first time. But if 'ee doant settle down at the Manor, why come back whoam to the farm. 'Ee can always start again somewheers else.'

This practical advice cheered me up immensely, and by the time we had jogged our slow way to the Manor and driven into the cobbled yard at the back of the big house, my tears had quite vanished.

A number of men, grooms and stablehands, were laughing and talking together when we drove in. The lint-haired lad I had seen on my first visit, detached himself from the group and came towards us, staring at me with great interest. His hair was even more untidy than it had been on that first occasion, but his eyes were blue and merry and young, and his grin infectious, and my heart warmed towards him. I smiled shyly at him as Ben rang the bell, and he looked as if he were going to speak to me; but before he could do so, the door was opened by a tall girl in a pink print dress and a cap and apron. Ben put my trunk and the holdall in the narrow passage into which the door opened. Then, with an encouraging pat on my shoulder, he departed, leaving me alone, feeling dreadfully forlorn, beside the tall girl.

From inside Mrs. Beck's sitting-room I could hear her voice, sharp with annoyance, scolding someone.

'Now get about your work and see you do it properly, and don't let me have to speak to you again!' she shrilled, and the girl who was being scolded came out of the room. She was a pretty little body with a round rosy face and lips that were meant to laugh and be gay, but she looked far from gay at the moment. She was scowling and her lips were set together in a hard tight line as though she was holding back a sharp retort. She glanced at me, and then ran down the passage and disappeared through a green baize door which led, as I later found, to the kitchen regions. Mrs. Beck came out of the room, apparently hot on her heels, but seeing me the house-keeper stopped and surveyed me.

'Oh, so you've come!' she said, and her brows elevated themselves as her glance travelled from my bonnet and my new dress to the neat black laced boots on my feet.

'You're rather too much the young madam in your dress, my girl,' she said. 'And so I shall tell your grandmother the next time I see her. However spoilt you may have been at home, here you're just another maid—the kitchen-maid, the least important one at that, and don't you forget it! I hope the rest of your clothes are more suitable to your place than these—I sent your grandmother a list.'

I stammered out that my grandmother had read the list, and that I was sure she would

15

find my working clothes all that they should be. Mrs. Beck shrugged her shoulders discontentedly, commented that she would have a look at them when she could spare the time, and bade the tall girl, who was standing silently by, help me to carry my trunk up to the attic bedroom where I was to sleep.

The sitting-room door closed behind the lean, black-clad figure, and the tall girl, suddenly unbending, smiled at me, and taking one of the handles of my trunk helped me to drag it towards the back stairs. As we were struggling to get the trunk round the bend of the staircase, the kitchen door opened, a grinning, freckled face peered cautiously through, and then the lint-haired boy came after us.

'You girls want a hand with that?' he said. And without more ado, he shouldered my trunk and carried it lightly up the steep stairs. The tall girl, whose name, I discovered, was Mary, and I followed him with my holdall, Mary protesting all the way that Johnny oughtn't to come up to the attics where the girls slept, and how on earth had he managed to slip through the kitchen—he knew he was never allowed there except for meals. Johnny cocked a mischievous eye at me over his shoulder and winked.

'Don't you go paying too much heed to our

16

Mary,' he said. 'She's always on the jump. She ought to be like me and take a scolding like a duck takes water—shake it off me back and forget it!'

I laughed. It was difficult not to like this fresh-faced youngster. As he dumped the trunk down in the long attic room in which I was to sleep, and then ran off with a grin and a 'go on, it's nought,' in answer to my shy thanks, I felt, with a warm and pleasant feeling, that I had found someone who was going to be a friend.

Mary looked after his disappearing figure with some disapproval.

'He's a saucebox if ever there was one, that Johnny Bligh,' she said. 'But he's got a good heart, I will say that for him. We'd never have got that trunk of yours upstairs by ourselves.'

We spent the next half-hour unpacking my things, Mary commenting admiringly on Mrs. Nudd's fine stitching and saying enviously that I must have a kind pair of grandparents to fit me out so generously. Then the shrill sound of a bell made her depart in haste, warning me, as she went, to put on my gingham gown and my cap and apron as quickly as I could and then come down to the kitchen to meet Mrs. Dibben the cook and the other servants and have tea.

17

I made myself ready, lingering as long over the operation as I dared, for I was overcome with shyness—and was dismayed, too, at the thought of sharing a bedroom with three other girls. At home on the farm I had my own little room, and though my grandmother had warned me that I should probably have to share sleeping-quarters with others, I felt very depressed now that I was faced with it in reality. The attic was long and narrow, with a heavily-beamed roof that sloped down all along one side. It was dark, for it was lighted by only two small dormer windows, and the four iron bedsteads that faced them were very narrow. Three of the beds were carefully made, with coloured cotton coverlets drawn over them, but the fourth bed was still dishevelled, although it was four o'clock in the afternoon, with bedclothes all awry, and on the floor an untidy litter of garments. There were some hooks for clothes set into the oak beams which here and there ran along the walls, and a row of ricketty bookshelves which, instead of books, held a clutter of hairbrushes, grease pots and combs. The maids who occupied the room were evidently expected to keep most of their things inside their boxes, which were ranged along the wall opposite to the beds, for there was nothing in the shape of a press or wardrobe or chest-of-drawers.

It was with a very sober face that I at last
nerved myself to descend the steep stairs,
push open the green baize door, and walk into
the great kitchen. The entire staff, it seemed
to me, were sitting at tea at the long kitchen
table, though, later on, I found that some of
the upper servants had their meals apart from
the rest of us, and the butler, Mr. Lord, a
dignified old man, stout in build and perfectly
bald, took his with Mrs. Beck in her private
sitting-room. On the day on which I arrived,
my lord and lady were entertaining guests to
tea, and so the tall footmen, Henry and
Edgar, were absent, serving upstairs. Normally, they sat at the right and left of Mrs.
Dibben at the head of the table, while the rest
of the staff, arranged according to their
standing, spread down each side to the
bottom, where I saw an empty place, the
humblest, waiting for me. The entire staff
turned to stare at me as I entered, and I stood
there, scarlet with embarrassment, wishing
that the earth would open and swallow me up.

Then an impatient voice came from the end
of the room, the voice of Mrs. Dibben, the
cook.

'That the new girl? You're late, Emily
Skeffington. Still, as it's your first day, we'll

forget it for once. Sit down and have your tea, it's half over as it is.'

I slid hastily into the vacant chair, and found myself sitting between the lint-haired boy, Johnny Bligh, and a small girl with rosy cheeks and red-brown eyes like a squirrel— the girl I had seen leaving Mrs. Beck's room when I arrived. The tall girl, called Mary, smiled and pushed a plate of buttered scones towards me, and Johnny handed a jar of raspberry jam to me, murmuring:

'Go on, have some. It's good.'

The rosy-cheeked girl beside me turned towards me.

'So you're Emily Skeffington, are you?' she said. 'Bad luck having a name like that! Skeffington—Skivvy! And that's what you are— a skivvy like the rest of us.'

I stared at her.

'Skivvy? What do you mean?' I asked.

'It's what some of the upstair folk call us maids,' Mary said with a curl of her lip. 'Some say "slavey," which is just as bad. Nice names for us who work for them like slaves, while they spend money and loaf about doing nothing all day long.'

Johnny cocked his tousled head at her and grinned.

'You're talking radical!' he told her. 'It's

not for the likes of us to sit in judgment on our betters—as Mrs. Dibben's always telling us. Especially not young skivvies like Emily.'

'I don't want to be called Skivvy,' I protested. 'My name's Skeffington, though you can call me Emily or Emmie, if you like.'

The rosy-cheeked girl laughed in half-humorous contempt.

'You won't be asked what you're called,' she commented. 'You'll be Skivvy from now on—it comes too easy.'

She turned away from me to converse with her other neighbour, and I sat, mute as a mouse, studying those about me, and wondering how long it would be before I disentangled one from another, and what I should be expected to do. One thing seemed obvious, and when I had done eating and the others were leaving the table, I took my courage in both hands, went up to Mrs. Dibben, and asked if I should help with the washing-up. She was still seated, having her tea, and she looked up at me and eyed me keenly, but kindly enough. She had a sharp tongue, had Mother Dibben, but she was a good soul at heart, and I never had cause to complain of her treatment of me. In which I was luckier than I then realized—too many cooks in those days made life sheer hell for their kitchenmaids.

'Wash-up? Yes, of course, and look sharp about it. There's no call to dirty that nice clean apron though. Take it off and put on a sacking one—there's one behind the scullery door.'

Then, as I turned towards the door in question, she went on:

'You're Nan Skeffington's granddaughter, ain't you? You don't token your Ma any. She was fair, and pretty as a picture. You'll never set men's heads turning the way Minnie did, though you ain't bad as dark ones go. Likely you take after your dad. I never saw him myself, but they say he was a good-looker, even if he was a rogue.'

She surveyed me up and down, while I grew redder and redder until I was almost on the point of bursting into tears. Then with a laugh she rose to her feet, and slapped me on the back, saying:

'There, there, child! Don't take on. Be a good lass and work hard and do as you're bid, and you'll come to no harm. Away with you now, and do those dishes.'

'Please,' I stammered, 'C-could somebody show me where to put away the things when I've washed them?'

'Well, if I'm not a noddy! Of course you'll

need someone to show you round this first night. Tilda! Stop your gossiping and come and give a hand to the new girl with the washing-up. I'm going now for my snooze, and one of you can wake me at six. Thank the Lord it's Sunday and a cold supper!'

She stumped out of the kitchen, and a girl detached herself from the bunch of girls giggling together by the window. It was the rosy-cheeked girl—so she was Tilda. Her pretty little face wore a discontented expression as she led the way into the scullery. Then she nodded back towards the kitchen.

'Bring in the dishes, young Skivvy,' she commanded. 'I'll help you this once, since the old cow's told me to, but *only* this once, mind. But Ma Dibben didn't tell me to carry all those plates and things out here, so *you* can do that—and when you've brought them all in, we'll wash up.'

Tilda was only three years my elder, but to me she seemed much more than that, and without a word I brought in all the dirty crockery. Later on, Johnny Bligh often used to perform this task, but that first evening I trudged back and forth between the kitchen table and the scullery at least a dozen times, while Tilda sat and watched me with a gleam of amusement in her eyes. We did the

23

washing-up and she showed me where everything was kept, and in the casual talk with
which we beguiled our work I discovered that
she was the owner of the unmade bed in the
attic—Mary and a girl called Jane, were the
occupants of the other two beds. I must admit
that Tilda showed me round thoroughly, and
though, in the end, I could not have said
whether I liked or disliked her, I found her an
amusing companion. She was a born mimic,
and could take off anybody. She had an aunt
on the Halls, she told me, and had wanted to
go on them herself, but her parents wouldn't
hear of her doing so. So here she was—a
Skivvy like me!

I may say here that though this nickname
annoyed me very much at first, I could not
avoid it, and after awhile I grew so used to it
that I ceased to mind it—in fact, I rather
liked it in the end!

Tilda had no intention of remaining a
skivvy all her life—not she! When I asked her
what she planned to do instead, she became
evasive. She wasn't sure—but one thing was
certain. She didn't mean to stay in service any
longer than she could help. Stilwell Manor for
her was only a jumping-off place.

I was so interested in her chatter that she
became more friendly, and after everything

was washed and put away we went upstairs together and I showed her my new clothes, and helped her to make her bed and tidy up her end of the room. Then we tidied ourselves to go downstairs to supper. Tilda's eyes fastened on me as I was putting a brooch into my collar.

'I like that,' she said. 'Cameo isn't it? I've got a pair of cameo ear-rings that was my granny's, but I can't wear 'em without a brooch to match.'

On an impulse, I held out my cameo brooch.

'You can have this,' I said grandly. 'I've got several other brooches I can use. I can spare this one.'

Tilda seized the brooch greedily and burst into effusive thanks. She loved it—she would always wear it—she had guessed from her first sight of me that we were going to be friends! We went down to supper arm-in-arm, and she helped me again with the washing-up, and the last thing I heard that night when I was in bed was Tilda's voice bidding me sleep well and saying again, for the fifth or sixth time, how glad she was that we were friends.

Were we? For the life of me I couldn't tell, then or ever, whether or not I really liked Tilda Harman. There was something about her that drew me, that held us together from that time on, so that to the outer world we seemed to be friends—great friends. If I had known then what the future held for us! If I had only known!

CHAPTER THREE

I GET PROMOTED

IT WAS some days before I saw Lady Stilwell, and during those days I learnt more about hard work than I had ever thought was to be known. Six o'clock was the hour for rising in summer and seven in the winter; but as Mrs. Dibben liked a cup of tea to be brought to her in bed, I had to get up a quarter of an hour earlier so as to make it and bring it to her. I used often to steal a cup from the pot I made for her, especially when the cold weather came and I was shivering as I lit the fire in the huge black stove, holding a sheet of newspaper in front of it to get it started quickly. After lighting the stove and taking Mrs. Dibben her tea, my duties were to sweep and dust the kitchen, scullery, larder, and the narrow hall that ran from the green baize door to the back entrance. Twice a week I had to wash down the three stone steps outside the door and polish the brass handle, door-knocker, and letter box.

After these jobs were done, I was supposed to lay the table ready for the staff's breakfast, set the kettle to boil, and get my lady's tray ready, and the tray for Miss Angela and her nurse. My other duties were too numerous to mention, and I was so busy learning them the first three or four days that I never got out of the house at all, not even for a breath of fresh air, though it was lovely weather and in between dusting, and washing, and sweeping, I used to look longingly at the sunshine outside and wish that I could slip out into it, even if only for half-an-hour. So my delight can be imagined when one Sunday afternoon Mrs. Dibben said to me that as there wasn't much to be prepared for supper, since it was to be all cold, I might go with Tilda into the kitchen garden and gather strawberries to make into jam. We were not to eat any of the strawberries, Mrs. Dibben said, but there would be strawberries and cream for the staff at supper that night, and if we picked well, we two might get an extra large helping.

I called Tilda, who came willingly enough, but she sniffed scornfully when I told her of Mrs. Dibben's prohibition.

'Maybe you were fool enough to promise for yourself, but you didn't promise for *me*,' she said. 'There's nothing to stop me from taking a berry here and there if I want to— and if you dare give me away—'

I told her that I wasn't in the habit of telling tales, and she laughed and we took two big baskets apiece and went towards the kitchen garden. It lay behind the house, a great walled square with netted enclosures where the soft fruits grew. As we went in I saw three figures beside the strawberry beds—my lady with her little girl and the nurse, and my heart leapt with excitement. At last I was going to see her again, the pretty lady of my childhood. Knowing that Tilda would laugh at me, I hid my excitement as best I could, and made no reply to Tilda's annoyed exclamation.

'Drat it! There's my lady! Of all the bad luck!'

Hearing our footsteps on the path, Lady Stilwell turned and looked at us. For a moment, as her eyes fell upon me, she looked puzzled, then her face cleared and she smiled.

'Why, it's little Emily Skeffington,' she said. 'Though you aren't so little any more now, are you! What a difference it makes putting your hair up—I hardly knew you.'

She smiled kindly at Tilda.

'I know *you*, though, well enough! You look after the nursery,' she said to her. Then she turned to me again, and my heart was dancing.

'I hope you are happy here, Emily? I promised your good grandmother that you should be.'

'Oh, yes, my lady! I wouldn't be anywhere else but here, not for the world, my lady! I wouldn't, indeed!' I said in a rush.

She laughed, and her laugh ran like a silver echo through the sleepy warmth of the old garden.

'That's good. I hope you will continue to like us. I hear from Mrs. Beck that you are working very well. You have come out to pick strawberries? Well, you had better get on with it. Don't eat too many as you pick, though of course you may have a few. Come Angela, you have eaten enough and it is time for your afternoon sleep.'

With another smile at us she turned away, and I stood and watched her as she held out her hand to her little girl and walked slowly along the path towards the gate, the nurse following demurely behind. How lovely she was, I thought, and I stood gazing after her, bemused, until I was aroused by Tilda's elbow digging into my side.

'Come on! What are you doing? Mooning like that after my lady?' she demanded. 'You never seen a fine lady before that you've got to gape after her like a country lout?'

I turned to my picking without making any reply, and for awhile we worked in silence. Presently, as our baskets began to fill with the juicy crimson berries, Tilda began to talk again—she was one who could never keep silent for long.

'Pity she can't have a boy, isn't it? That Angela's her only child. If she doesn't have a boy, the whole place will go to a distant cousin when my lord dies.'

I was startled.

'Will it?' I said, and in a minute Tilda was off on a long discourse about estates and inheritance and the laws concerning the ownership of property, all of which was new to me. I had never thought much about the lives and ways of great folk, but Tilda, whose great ambition was to rise above the class in which she was born, had gone to some trouble to learn about the life she longed to enter. For quite a long time, as we stooped over the strawberry beds, she expounded her views on the subject. I listened, deeply interested, because it touched so closely the woman who fascinated me so, and at last put a question. Tilda straightened her aching back, slipped a strawberry into her mouth, and nodded.

'Oh, yes, she had a boy. But it died at birth. Didn't live but a minute. And she's had a miscarriage or two, as well, that might have been boys. That Angela's the only one that lived, and she doesn't look more than a weedy little piece to me.'

'How dreadfully disappointed she must have been when the boy baby died,' I said.

'They say she cried day and night for weeks,' Tilda said with relish. 'Can't think why she can't throw stronger babies! Maybe it's *his* fault—too long and lean. If I was married and it happened to me, I'd try somebody else, I would, and see if he couldn't get me a stronger baby.'

I looked at her in horror.

'But that would be adultery!' I cried. 'Oh, no—'

'Oh, yes!' mimicked Tilda. 'What a simpleton you are sometimes, Emily. Of course it 'ud be adultery, but who would know or care if the baby came off all right? There's many a fine lady's fathered another man's child on her husband—and if it meant getting an heir to all this it would be worth it!'

I didn't like what she was saying, but I understood how she felt. Would *any* price be too high to pay to retain this splendid heritage—the Manor, the gardens, the green parkland with its magnificent trees, the river, the lake, the fields—for one's son and one's

32

son's sons? Yet Tilda's suggestion in connection with my lady revolted me, and I turned away and picked up my baskets.

'Come on,' I said, over my shoulder. 'It's getting late, it must be nearly supper-time.' And Tilda picked up her baskets, and we hurried off, and no more was said about an heir to the Manor.

*   *   *

For the first few weeks at the Manor, I was too busy getting used to my new life to have time to feel homesick. But when I got used to my work, I must admit that there were times when I felt like a forlorn little stranger in a new world, and longed for my grandmother and grandfather, and all the friends on the farm with whom I had spent my childhood. As the summer passed away and was succeeded by autumn and I learnt that I was not, as I had hoped, to be allowed to spend Christmas at home, my spirits sank very low, indeed. But it was no use grumbling, and I did my best to look cheerful and not let anyone know how miserable I was feeling.

Christmas was to be a gay and busy time at the Manor, with people staying and all sorts of parties going on, and we should all be

33

needed to do the work. After Christmas, if we were good girls and did our work well, we might perhaps, Mrs. Dibben said, be allowed in turn to spend a couple of days with our families. That, of course, was better than nothing, but to me it was little enough compared with the happy Christmas at the farm for which I had hoped, and I shed a few tears as I stitched away at some mending I had on hand for Miss Angela. She was then ten years old and had become something of a romp, and I had felt very proud when my lady, talking one day to Mrs. Beck about engaging a sewing woman to come in once or twice a week to see to the little girl's clothes, had suddenly said:

'But what am I thinking of! There's no need to bring in anybody from outside. That child Emily Skeffington is a wonderful needlewoman—I've seen some of her work at her grandmother's. Arrange for her to do any fine mending needed on my own or Miss Angela's things. That will be much better than engaging anyone extra.'

I had heard this conversation, for it was Tilda's day off, and I had carried up the tray with tea for Miss Angela and her nurse. There was a table outside the nursery where one could rest a tray while one opened the door, and I had just put the tray down and was waiting for a moment to get my breath after climbing the stairs from the kitchen, when I saw my lady and Mrs. Beck standing with their backs to me at the other end of the passage, and I couldn't help hearing what they were saying. I was struck all of a heap, as the saying is, with surprise and delight at the idea of being allowed to do my lady's mending, and I held my breath as I listened for Mrs. Beck's reply. There was a dubious note in her voice when she spoke.

'Well, of course, my lady, if you *wish* it, it can be arranged. It will mean that Emily won't be able to do so much in the kitchen, and I don't quite know what Mrs. Dibben will say—'

My lady interrupted her impatiently.

'What does it matter what Mrs. Dibben says? Get her another kitchenmaid for the rough work if she needs one. Kitchenmaids are much easier to find than good sewing-maids. Get one, anyway, because if Emily is going to handle my clothes, her hands mustn't be allowed to get rough and coarse.'

'I could get another young girl easily enough,' Mrs. Beck conceded. 'Perhaps I could move the girls up a step, all of them. Mary's leaving to get married, and I could move Jane into her place and Tilda into

Jane's. That would make Emily under-housemaid, and I could see that her duties are arranged to leave time for her to do the mending. Would that suit your ladyship?'

My lady was already descending the main staircase, and her voice floated back to me.

'Really, I don't mind how you arrange it, as long as Emily is available whenever anything of mine or Miss Angela's needs mending. Of course, she must have a rise in her wages. Give her what Tilda's getting now—that will be fair.'

For the rest of that day I walked about in a dream. Here was something to make up for my lost Christmas. Promoted from kitchen-maid to under-housemaid in less than six months. A Christmas present, indeed!

That was how my first 'step' came, and thanks to it my Christmas was far happier than I had expected.

It was that Christmas that I saw my first Christmas-tree. In those days one did not see one in every house as one does now, and I felt very excited about it. It was cut on the estate where there was a plantation of fir trees, and was brought into the house by the gardeners and set up in a big tub, filled with wet sand. The tub and the sand were hidden with greenery, and my lady and her sister, Lady

Amperley, who was spending Christmas at the Manor, with Mrs. Beck and some of the upper servants, decorated it and hung presents on it.

After it was done, Mrs. Beck locked the door, for there was to be a big children's party on Christmas Day and the tree was to be kept hidden until then. But my lady, who was always so kind to us girls, gave permission for us to go and look at it just before the young ladies and gentlemen invited to the party went in, and I must say that when I saw it all lit up and glittering with tinsel streamers and artificial frost and with its tiny candle flames flickering in the draught, I gaped like a countryman on his first visit to London, and thought it was the prettiest thing I had ever seen.

I had to help get Miss Angela and her two young cousins, Lady Amperley's children, dressed for the party, and then, as some of the guests were already arriving, Nurse Haversham and I took them downstairs and the party started. Nurse Haversham kept me with her in case any help was needed with the younger visitors, and we stood against the door, watching while my lady and her sister handed out the presents which the two tall footmen reached down for them from the tree. The plan had been that when the present-giving was over, the children should all troop down to the dining-room for tea, where Miss Angela would cut the first slice of the Christmas cake, crackers would be pulled, carols sung, and the party end in a dazzle of jollity. The party ended in a dazzle all right— but of a different sort to what had been planned!

Most of the presents had been taken off the tree, and some of the worst din of blowing of trumpets and banging of drums had died down, when I caught sight of something that made my heart turn over. Miss Angela, stooping over a toy she had found tied to one of the lower branches which had somehow been overlooked, moved just a little too close to one of the lighted candles. I rushed forward to pull her back, but I was just a split second too late. The flame caught a strand of her long hair, worn loose as the fashion was for little girls in those days, and in a moment it flared up in a great burst of yellow fire!

She shrieked as the sharp pain seared her, and clapped her poor little hands to her head. Edgar, the second footman who was picking up bits of rubbish from the floor nearby, saw the flame blaze up the same moment as I did, and I heard him shout as I reached the child and threw my apron over her head, pressing it to me as tightly as I could to smother the fire. I wonder I didn't smother the child, too, while I was about it! But I was too agitated to think of anything but putting out the flames. I put them out all right—though my hands were burnt and there was a great hole in my apron (a brand new one sent to me as a Christmas present from my grandparents)—and I found myself, shaking all over, with Miss Angela still clutched in my arms, in the centre of a crowd of grown-ups, my lord and lady among them, clustering about me.

What happened then I can't quite remember, for I suddenly turned queer and had to sit down and be given a glass of brandy. But I think Lady Amperley and Nurse Haversham got the children away into the room where tea was laid and settled them down to the meal. When I came to myself again, I found that a doctor, who was luckily present at the party, was examining Miss Angela. He said that she had better be put to bed to recover from the shock she'd had, but actually, barring the loss of some of her hair and a slight scorch on one cheek which the doctor dressed, she had not suffered any severe hurt, thanks, he said, to my prompt action.

I found myself regarded as something of a heroine. My lady wept her gratitude and kissed me before them all, which made me most dreadfully embarrassed, wonderful as it was to feel her arms around me and her smooth scented cheek against my own. My lord, whose emotion seemed to make him almost as embarrassed as I was, contented himself by saying 'Good girl! Good girl!' at least a dozen times. One of the house party, who, I discovered afterwards, was my lord's cousin who would inherit the Stilwell estates failing a male heir in the direct line, inquired my name from Edgar and went and scribbled something in a corner, which Edgar gave me afterwards, and which turned out to be a cheque for five whole pounds! I had never seen a cheque before and I was thrilled. But when my lord sent me another cheque the next day I was very troubled and asked to see my lady.

She had just had her bath, and was still in her bedroom when I went to her. She turned from her dressing-table and smiled at me when her maid opened the door to my knock and I went in.

'Emily? I hope you slept well, my child, and that your hands don't hurt any more,' she said, as I went towards her. I could not speak, but I held out my lord's cheque, and my lady, realizing that I wanted to talk privately, sent her maid out of the room and then looked at me again.

'What is wrong, Emily?' she asked gently. 'You did us a great service last night, you know, a service that can never really be rewarded. We have given you that because we wanted to show you a little of the gratitude we feel.'

I really don't remember quite what I said. My hands were paining me a good deal in spite of the doctor's ointments and bandages, and I was still rather overwrought, I suppose from the excitement of the previous night. But somehow I managed to get out something of what I felt—that though I was grateful for the cheque my lord's cousin had given me and willing to accept it, I didn't feel the same about taking money from her and my lord for what, thanks to my being there at the right moment, I had been able to do. I didn't know why, but it felt *different*, somehow. No, I can't remember what I actually said, but my lady seemed to understand, and when I dissolved into tears, she put her arm round my shaking shoulders—that was the second time!—and kissed me and soothed me until I stopped crying.

'I think I know what you mean, Emily,' she said gently, 'and I appreciate the delicacy of your feelings. But you must try to understand, my child, that this is not just a kind of super-tip for a service rendered. One of these days you will want to marry—and every girl should have a little nest-egg in the Savings Bank ready for that day. My husband and I have talked it over, and we thought that if we gave you this to add to what Mr. Bruce-Orbyn has given you, it would make a good start towards it. Add what you can from your wages to it from time to time, and watch your savings grow bit by bit.'

That put a different complexion upon the matter, and I was ready now to accept the cheque with delight. I thanked my lady many times and begged her to thank my lord for me. The cheque was for ten pounds, so now I had fifteen pounds to put in the Savings Bank— more money than I had ever dreamt of possessing! I stitched both cheques up carefully inside the lining of my coat before I slept that night, and dreamt happily of the surprise and pleasure of my grandparents when I showed them my wealth.

NOTE BY SALLIE STILWELL

The MS here became so torn and dirty that we were unable to decipher any more for awhile. It was plain that the bundle of papers, as it grew, had been dragged hither and thither and hidden in all sorts of odd places. Some pages had been gnawed by mice and fell into bits when we touched them, while others were so damp-stained and crumpled that it was impossible to read them. Nearly three years seem to have passed when the manuscript became legible again 'Skivvy' had become sixteen, and she and Tilda were still friends. The old butler had died, and a new man had come to take his place. Few of the servants seemed to like him.

CHAPTER FOUR

SWEET SIXTEEN

I SPENT my sixteenth birthday, by kind permission of my lady, at the farm with my grandparents, and a very happy day it was. Looking back, I think it was the last truly happy day I was ever to know, for during the year that followed I lost my darling old grandfather. I lost something even more precious during that year, too—something no girl can ever replace once she has lost it!

My lady had been seriously ill the year before. It was another miscarriage and she had taken a long time to get over it. The doctors had shaken their heads and had said that she should not try to have another child. Yet everybody was sure that she *would* try, for apart from wanting to please my lord, who naturally wanted an heir, she herself longed passionately for a son, and, as I know now, prayed for one unceasingly. She continued to show me the greatest possible kindness, even in her weakness, and learning by accident that my birthday was near, she insisted that I must have the day off on it.

I remember that it was on that day, while I was sitting with my grandmother, holding some wool for her to wind, that I first noticed that she was ageing. I saw with something like surprise how lined was her face, and how faded were her once keen blue eyes. She caught me looking at her and laughed a little sadly.

'Thinking how old I am, eh lass?' she said, and I flushed—it was uncanny how often my shrewd grandmother would guess what I was thinking. She went on, winding busily as she talked.

'Yes, I'm getting on, and so's your grandfather, bless him! But nobody can live for ever, and when my time comes, Emily, I'll go with a contented heart, for I've set your feet on a straight path and with God's help you won't leave it. I'm glad you've got a bit put by in the Savings Bank, for that's always a good thing. There'll be a little money to come to you when we die, and in my will I've left you enough furniture, china, and linen, to set up a little home for yourself sometime. We can't leave you the farm. It needs a man to run it, and anyway your grandfather has set his heart on leaving it to his nephew, Shem Skeffington. You remember him?'

I nodded. I remembered him, a large, shy

45

young man with fiery red hair. A good-hearted fellow enough, but I'd never felt attracted to him, though I knew that he more than liked me. He had spoken to my grand-father about our getting married, and I knew I'd disappointed everybody by refusing to think of him in that way.

'It's a thousand pities you couldn't bring yourself to fancy Shem,' said my grand-mother rather acidly as I remained silent. 'He's a good fellow and one of the best far-mers here-abouts. With his farm joined to ours, he'll be the biggest farmer in the district. You'd be right well off if you were his wife. But there 'tis—you'll go your own way, I sup-pose. Is there anyone around the Manor who's taken your fancy? What about that light-haired lad, Johnny Bligh?'

I laughed and reddened again. Johnny Bligh had been my persistent admirer ever since I came to the Manor. But he was a shy lad, and I was shy, too, and though we liked each other and were good friends, we were nothing more—at least, at that time. During the past year, in which I had blossomed out into young womanhood, more than one of the men servants at the Manor had begun to notice me. I was never really pretty, that I know, but I was young and healthy and well-grown, and though I was never a magnet to men the way my mother had been, I can't say I didn't have my admirers—as many of them, anyway, as is good for a girl.

'Oh, I like Johnny very much,' I said. 'But I don't want to marry him, and anyhow he hasn't asked me. One or two of the others have tried to kiss me, but—'

I stopped, and my grandmother laughed drily.

'As long as it stops at a kiss, there's no harm done,' she said. 'But mind you, a kiss is sometimes a spark that lights a fire, so be careful, my lass. What's the new butler like—him that's taken the place of the old man?'

I frowned.

'Mr. Valentine? He's only been with us a month and it's hard to tell. He's very good at his work and keeps everybody up to the mark, and my lord and lady seem to like him.'

'What sort of age is he?' my grandmother asked.

'I don't know. I should think about forty or a bit over. He's tall and well built, and speaks smoothly enough, but I don't like his eyes.' I hesitated and giggled at the memory. 'But Mrs. Beck likes him well enough! She's setting her cap at him, for all she must be years older than he is. She's using powder on her face, and some red stuff—at least Tilda says she is, and she waits on Mrs. Beck, you know, and knows all about her.'

'That Tilda's a gossip. I'm not at all sure she's a good friend for you,' said my grandmother. 'She'd ought to've got higher than second housemaid by now. You've done better than she has, though she's been at the Manor longer than you by several years.'

I said nothing. Loyalty, and a queer sort of affection that I had developed for Tilda stopped my making any comment, though I could have given a pretty accurate guess at the reason she was not promoted as she should have been. She was too fond of the men! She was forever up to the neck in some love affair or other. She was a pretty girl, full of fun and laughter, and she attracted men all right, but her affairs never came to anything in the end, for after awhile the men realized that even when they were kissing her, she had a spare eye over their shoulder for some other fellow—and that doesn't lead to a man asking a girl to be his wife. She did her work well, so was kept on, but both Mrs. Beck and Mrs. Dibben dubbed her 'flighty,' and that meant she couldn't be trusted with a position as responsible as parlourmaid, or even head housemaid, both of which jobs called for a steadiness and dignity which Tilda would never have.

She was candid about her love affairs to me, and she had plenty of opportunity to tell me about them, for now we shared a room together on our own. The sleeping arrangements had been altered for us girls. A second attic had been cleared in another wing of the big house, so now instead of sleeping four in a room there were only two of us—me and Tilda in one, and two other girls in the other. When we were moving the junk out of the second attic, we came upon a thing that I think was called a 'brazier.' My lady's maid, who was helping us, had done a lot of travelling and she said that in countries abroad it was filled with hot coals and used to warm the big cold rooms in Italian palaces. It stood on legs and had a handle so that it could be carried about, and the sides had holes pierced in them.

It was Tilda who thought of using it, I wouldn't have dared! But one cold night she brought it to our room, stood it on a big iron tray she had sneaked from the kitchen, and then lighted a fire in it. I was scared at first, for I knew we should get into shocking trouble if we were caught. But I couldn't help enjoying the warmth of it, and from that time onward we used regularly to smuggle up bits of coal in our pails or in our pockets, which we wrapped up in paper and kept in a wooden sugar box. There was little risk really that we would be found out, for the two older girls never came into our bedroom, and neither Ma Dibben nor Mrs. Beck would ever dream of climbing all the stairs up to our attic. Mrs. Dibben was too fat, and Mrs. Beck too grand, and anyway, she was far too taken up with the new butler, Mr. Valentine, to bother about what we did in our bedrooms when work was over.

Valentine was popular with the men servants, for he had a fund of smutty stories that amused them. Once when he was in the kitchen he began to talk that way in front of all of us. But Mrs. Dibben shut him up with a snap, and told him that if he came into her kitchen she'd thank him to keep a clean tongue in his head. He looked at her with his head on one side, and said smoothly: 'Of course, Mrs. Dibben. I apologize—for the moment I got carried away.' But his narrow eyes looked at her like a snake's, filled with hate.

He *was* rather like a snake—or maybe a cat. Sleek and sort of insinuating. I think he must have worn rubber soles on his shoes, for he could walk more quietly than anybody I ever knew and many's the time one of the girls would jump and scream to find him standing at her elbow when she'd thought him miles away. Not that they minded that! All of them, except Mrs. Dibben and me, thought he was wonderful, and would have given the eyes out of their silly heads to have him take notice of them. Not that he ever did. He was all for setting himself up with Mrs. Beck—or maybe with the money she had put away—and he took no notice of us girls except for giving us orders or just passing the time of day. Tilda, who'd tried hard to get him to make eyes at her, gave it up at last and said angrily that she didn't believe he was a man at all.

As a matter of fact, as he told me afterwards, the eagerness of the girls to attract him put him off. He was the kind of man who wanted to do the hunting, not to be hunted, and it was chiefly because I was the only one who never took any notice of him that he started to be interested in me. That—and the fact that I had a good figure, as I couldn't help knowing, and possessed a certain poise and self-confidence and wasn't bad-looking in my way, made him, without my realizing it, take notice of me.

It was September, and Tilda was away on

51

holiday, and I had taken the opportunity to give our room a thorough cleaning. I had to do it at night, of course, for I had Tilda's work as well as my own to do during the day. But when all my downstairs jobs were done and I had eaten my supper, I ran up to my bedroom, took off my clothes and slipped into my night-gown—it was a hot night, I remember, and I felt I'd be more comfortable working in that than in my daytime clothes—and set to to sweep and dust and make the attic really clean and shipshape.

I'm a fast worker and it didn't take me long to get the room straight. I had just finished and was washing my hands at the washstand, which, now that there was room for more furniture, Lady Stilwell had had put in the attic for us, when I heard a light tap at the door. Thinking it was Biddy, the girl who had taken my place in the kitchen, I called out 'Come in,' and went on washing without looking round. I heard somebody enter the room, and, still without looking, I said:

'Sit down on the bed, Bid, I won't be a minute.'

There was no reply, and I swung round—and then gasped. Mr. Valentine was sitting on the edge of my bed, smiling blandly at me. For a moment I simply stood and stared, quite at a loss to understand why he should be there. He had never before shown any special interest in me, like other fellows had done when they wanted me to notice them. He'd never winked at me, or squeezed my hand, or jostled me in a passage, or made any excuse to sit next to me at table, or anything like that. As for me, though I couldn't help but admire him, for he was a good-looking man, I had never thought of him as anything else but Mr. Valentine the butler—someone so far above me that I had never dreamt of thinking of him as on the same level as myself, as I thought of my merry friend, Johnny Bligh. So I just stood and stared, and it was he at last who broke the silence.

'Well, young Emmie, I've come to visit you.'

At the sound of his voice, I woke to the realization that I only had on my nightgown, and I made a dive for my dressing-gown. But that was a fatal move, for it was lying on my bed, and my plunge towards it brought me within reach of his arm. He seized my wrist, and with an expert twist brought me on to the bed, right on to his knees!

I struggled madly, but he gripped my legs together between his and pinioned my arms to my sides. Then he looked down at me and laughed as I writhed and panted. I didn't want to scream, for if anyone had heard me and come along and found a man in my bedroom it would have meant a terrible scandal and probably my dismissal—besides I doubted if there was anyone within hearing, for most of the maids were away on holiday, and the attic I was in overlooked the front of the house, and all the stablemen's quarters were round at the back. So I fought him in silence, though even then I did not really know what I was in for. I soon knew, though. My struggles evidently excited him, for suddenly he clutched me so tight that I couldn't move, and clamped his mouth over mine in a kiss the like of which I had never experienced before.

I'm not going to deny that I'd exchanged quite a few kisses, here and there, with Johnny or one of the other lads in the stables, or out in the woodlands when I was wandering there on my days off. But there is all the difference in the world between the shy, blundering kisses of a boy, and the kisses of a man who knows his way about with women. I'd never in my life known a kiss like that— horrifying at first, then suddenly thrilling, turning all one's body limp with sheer desire.

God knows how long that kiss lasted! All I

know is that I emerged from it at last, dazed and quivering, to only find myself lying on my back on the bed, with my nightgown torn open and Valentine on the top of me. His face was close to mine, his mouth, too, and all I knew was that I wanted that mouth on mine again. In a daze, I heard his voice, hurried and hoarse with passion.

'I knew you were a virgin, Emmie. I knew it! I've watched you ever since I came and I meant to have you some day, to be the first with you. No, don't struggle my girl! You know you want me as much as I want you, and now I'm going to have you!'

Suddenly I realized what was going to happen. How could I lie supine, allowing myself to be raped by a man I scarcely knew and not make the least attempt to save myself? I must be mad! With a gigantic effort I tried to push him away and roll myself off the bed. But it was too late—and clapping one hand over my mouth so that I could not scream, he flung himself upon me.

It would be difficult to say just what my feelings were when I woke the next day and realized fully what had happened. I felt bitterly unhappy and ashamed and, as I went about my work, I wondered why I hadn't put up more of a fight, why I hadn't risked screaming, and a thousand other whys—and came to no conclusion. I was working by myself most of the day, which was a good thing, otherwise somebody might have noticed how glum and silent I was, for as a rule I was a cheerful sort of girl, always ready to laugh and chatter. But since my lady and Miss Angela were away at the time and I had no personal mending to do for them Mrs. Beck had set me to doing the linen, darning and patching sheets and tablecloths, turning in frayed edges and pulling together holes in lace and drawn-thread work. It was work that had to be done in the linen-room, so I was alone most of the while, and I was thankful for the solitude as I sat stitching by the window, mulling over in my mind the events of the night before and feeling thoroughly miserable.

Suddenly the door opened and Johnny Bligh's tousled head poked round it. I jumped, startled.

'Johnny!' I exclaimed. 'What are you doing here? You know you're not allowed above stairs except you're sent!'

'Well, that's all right. I've *been* sent.' Johnny came in and perched on the edge of the long table at which I was sitting. He grinned at me cheerfully, and miserable as I was I couldn't help smiling back, for Johnny at eighteen was one of those people you can't help liking, people who bring an atmosphere of kindness and happiness wherever they go.

He had grown into a pleasant-looking young man, my Johnny. I always called him that, and so did the others, for he was plainly in love with me, though as yet he had not said much about it. Balancing himself on the table, he held out a hand with a small parcel in it.

'For you,' he said, and for once his gay voice sounded discontented. 'A fairing—old Valentine's just come back from Guildford market and brought fairings for all the girls. Told me to bring this to you and say he hoped you'd like it.'

I took the parcel and opened it with an affectation of indifference. Johnny watched me, frowning—luckily his eyes were on my hands, not on my flushed face. The gift was nothing much—just a pretty little housewife to hold pins and needles and such like.

'That's very kind of Mr. Valentine,' I said. 'What did he give the others?'

'Oh, just ribbons and things. But you know, Em, I don't like that sly old devil giving you presents.'

'Oh, Johnny, don't be silly!' I said. 'Why,

he's old enough to be my father. He—he only means to be kind.'

'The old 'uns are often the worst,' Johnny said darkly. 'He watches his step here because he's out to catch old Beck and her savings. But he's one for the girls when he's out. I've heard of his goings-on in Guildford and other places.'

'Well, what's that to do with us?' I had picked up my stitching again as an excuse not to look at him. 'I don't care what he does in his time off, and you shouldn't either. It's no business of ours.'

'No—but *you're* business of *mine*,' Johnny said. 'I don't like the way the fellow looks at you when he thinks no-one is watching.'

'Oh, Johnny, don't be ridiculous!' I said, my cheeks on fire with embarrassment. 'I won't listen to such rubbish. If all you can do is to sit there and talk nonsense, you'd best go about your business and leave me to mine.'

Johnny slid off the table, and stood looking wistfully down at me, as I sat there with the rays of the setting sun—for it was almost supper time—slanting down on me. Then he blurted out:

'I wish you'd let it be *our* business, Em. Couldn't you? You know I want to marry you one, one day. I've got little enough to offer

58

you now—if I had more I'd have spoken sooner, for I've been in love with you a long time—ever since you drove in with your grandma and grandpa to see Mrs. Beck about a place here, I think. Let's get promised, Em, even though we have to wait awhile before we're wed?'

'Oh, Johnny,' I faltered. 'Please don't say any more. I can't—'

I got up to go, but as I rose Johnny's arms closed tight about me, and in a voice, husky with emotion, he said:

'Oh, Emmie! I do love you! Honest I do. Can't you love me just a little bit?'

Oh, dear Johnny! How little I knew you then, how little I appreciated you! It wasn't until years later, when I'd lost you, that I realized the depth and greatness of your love for me, the unselfishness of your nature, kindly and trustful, giving so much and asking so little in return. A bastard child, born in a workhouse, deserted even by his mother, flung on the unthinking world when he was barely out of the toddling stage—Johnny, my Johnny, was one of the great ones of the earth, and I never ceased to mourn him, though my full appreciation of him came too late.

His lips closed on mine in a kiss, warm,

loving, shy, and something within me wept to feel the innocence, the gentleness of it—so different from the fierceness of that evil kiss of last night. For a moment I lay motionless in Johnny's arms—then, with a sob, I pushed him away and ran to the door. I clattered down the stairs and Johnny followed me, smiling a little, for though I'd pushed him aside, I hadn't actually refused him, and that, for humble Johnny, was enough for the moment.

When the time came to go to bed that night, I didn't dare look at Mr. Valentine as I said good night to them all, and I ran upstairs like a hare to the refuge of my attic. Surely, I said to myself, he wouldn't come again. I'd lock myself in, and then he couldn't. But when I turned to do it, I saw that the key had gone. He had taken it with him when he left me in the early dawn, when the birds were beginning to cheep in the tree tops, and little Emmie Skeffington lay crying because she wasn't a maid any more, but had lost her virtue to a man who didn't care a button for her, except as a plaything for his lust.

I undressed in a sort of daze. I felt hopeless. There was nothing I could do, nowhere I could fly for refuge, no-one whom I dared to tell. There was nothing to do but wait with my heart in my mouth, hoping against hope that he would not come. But he came—and to my shame I neither fought nor screamed when he took me in his arms. There was no use in fighting—and, if I am to be honest, despite my fear and humiliation I felt a kind of shamed longing to know again the new and feverish sensation I had known the previous night.

Looking back now, I can understand what was the matter with me. With his devilish knowledge of women, Valentine aroused in me a passion I had not known I possessed, so that, for the time being, I lived for the nights when he came to me. When I think now about that time I feel most desperately ashamed, and puzzled, too, that I let things go on as I did without making any effort to stop them. If I had only had the courage to complain to Mrs. Dibben, or to my lady, I could have saved myself and got Valentine dismissed. Why *didn't* I? I didn't even *like* the man, much less love him! Yet somehow I couldn't resist him. Underneath all my fear and shame there ran that irresistible attraction, and I let him do with me whatever he would.

CHAPTER FIVE

MY SON IS BORN

IT IS strange that one never thinks of things like that happening to oneself—only to other people. Until I got to know that my lady was again expecting a baby, it never occurred to me that I might get caught that way myself. Maybe something inside me pushed the thought away whenever it started to come up, because, if I had faced up to things rightly, I might have stopped Valentine making love to me—and I didn't want to stop him! So when it happened I couldn't at first believe it! Me, Emily Skeffington, to be landed with a baby! And me only seventeen and without a husband!

I was simply stunned, and kept on telling myself that it must be all right. It *must* be! I managed to hide it from Tilda, thanks to my always being up before her and the fact that she always slept like a log which stopped her from hearing me when the morning sickness came along—as it did, though, thank God, that phase didn't last long. I was young and healthy, and took starting a baby in my stride.

Worse luck, in one way! I'd have been thankful then for some of my lady's delicacy so that I could have lost the thing easily—and yet, I don't know. I don't know! When there was no possibility of my fooling myself any longer, I told Valentine. He heard me out in silence, surveying me with eyes as hard as two stones, and when I'd done telling, he got up and stood jingling the coins in his pockets, a habit of his. A symptom, maybe, of his interest in the money he loved so well.

'Dammit! This would happen!' he said at last vexedly. His vexation was not for me, but for himself, that I knew. 'I'm not shouldering you for a permanency, young Emmie, with or without a baby, see? I'm marrying old Beck. It's all settled and she's giving in her notice in the spring. She's got a tidy sum put away and three cottages, all well let— and I'm not turning her down for you, so you needn't think it. The best thing you can do is to get rid of it.'

I stared at him.

'Get rid of it? But how?'

He frowned.

'I'd have thought a country girl 'ud know all sorts of ways. Herbs, roots—to bring things on or to shove 'em off,' he said with a sneer. 'If you don't, next time I go into

Guildford I'll get you something. Don't start weeping now! I hate women who snivel. It won't get in our way for ages yet, so come on, my girl!'

I could have got something to help me, I knew, from my grandmother, but I could not bring myself to tell her. The mere thought of doing so made me cringe with shame. Besides, I was sure that she would not do anything to stop the baby coming—it would have seemed utterly wrong to her. Once a child was conceived it was to her a living soul and had as much right to live as had all other souls. No, it would have been no use to ask her. As for the pills Valentine got for me, they did no good at all—only made me feel sick without helping me in the slightest!

So the weeks went by. My shape altered slowly, so slowly that, at times, I thought there was no change in me at all. I could see the change, though, in my lady as her delicate slenderness thickened and her gowns had to be let out more and more often as the child grew. She was so anxious to give the baby room that she would not allow her corsets to be laced up in the least tightly, and it was plain for all to see how happy she was at the prospect of becoming a mother again after so long a time and so many disappointments.

But as for myself, I laced myself up as tightly as I could, buying a new and extra-heavily boned pair of stays to make sure they were strong. Mercifully for me, skirts and aprons were worn full and bunchy round the hips just then, and I was no slender, delicately-built creature but a plump, sturdy body, so that it was unlikely that anyone would notice the thickening of my waistline.

I did my work in those weeks in a kind of blind desperation. Work acted as a drug to keep me from thinking, and I would do other people's jobs rather than sit still after supper, which was our usual leisure time. And then a sickening blow fell upon me—the loss of my dear old grandfather.

A man from the farm drove over with the news, and I was released at once to go to my grandmother. That was a nightmare journey for me—shaking with grief, and with fear, too, lest my grandmother should spy out my secret, despite my corsets and bunchy skirts. But I need not have feared. The shock had stunned her into an automaton that greeted me vaguely and then relapsed into staring, tearless silence unless anyone spoke to her directly.

She did not weep until after the funeral and we were back in the farmhouse. Then she

65

broke down and my Aunt Marion, her sister, put her to bed. I offered to stay for a night or two, but Aunt Marion was going to remain with her until she got over the shock, and there was no need for me to be there as well. When I went to say good-bye to her, she realized who I was—I don't think she really had, before—and she cried as she kissed me and hugged me and made me promise to come and see her again soon. I thought over my promise as I jogged back to the Manor in the farm cart, and my heart was very heavy. What hope would I have of concealing my state from her in even a short time? The only chance would be to wait until it was all over—then, with my burden removed, I might risk another visit.

But what could I do with the baby when it came? Where could I go to have it in the first place? I had been lucky so far, for nobody seemed to have the least suspicion about me as yet, though Johnny had teased me a little for putting on weight. But that was understandable with the lavish meals we had at the Manor, and I pretended a great appetite for cream and butter to give colour to the idea that I was growing fat from over-eating.

So time drifted on until one night I woke up with a sudden grinding pain in my stomach. I did not realize at first what it was and called out 'Tilda! Tilda!' and Tilda, who for once had been sleeping lightly, woke up and came across the room to my bedside. She pulled the sheets off me, stared for a moment, then flung the coverings over me again with a brusque:

'Just as I thought—the kid's coming!'

She hurried to the corner where we kept the brazier, stuffed paper, wood, and coal, into it and lighted a fire. Then she got an old kettle which we also had in the room, filled it with water from the jug on the washstand and set it on to boil. Watching her, I said feebly:

'So you know?'

'Yes. I guessed some time ago when I caught a sight of you standing sideways in your nightgown without your stays. I must say you've been pretty clever, Skivvy, keeping it to yourself so long. It must be coming early, or you'd never have been able to hide it by now.'

I groaned. The pains were coming again.

'Don't—tell?' I jerked out between the spasms of pain.

'Don't be a fool!' said Tilda. 'Think I want to see you chucked out—the only girl I've ever got on with in this hole of a place? Don't you worry. I've helped my mother see my two sisters through their birthings, and there's nothing I don't know about it. Only thing is, I shall have to tear up one of your old night-gowns to use as rags for the blessed kid when it comes—mine are all dirty. I'll do every-thing—but for goodness sake try not to yell out and bring the others round to see what's happening.'

Tilda was as good as her word. Through pain such as I had never dreamed of, I was dimly aware of her competent hands about me and of her whispered words of cheer as the pains came faster and faster. I stifled my cries by stuffing a corner of the sheet into my mouth—afterwards I found that I had bitten that corner into shreds. At last I must have blacked out completely, for when again I came to myself Tilda was sitting beside me with a red, wrinkled, scrap of humanity on her lap, washing it carefully with a piece of my torn nightgown.

She grinned at me triumphantly as she met my eyes, and held up the newly-born child. And by the light of a flickering candle I looked my first upon my son.

Whatever might be said about Tilda later on in life, at that time she was a godsend to me, and to the little mewling thing that had come so prematurely into the world—two whole months too early, as we reasoned things

68

out. But though the child was tiny, he was perfectly formed and able to cry—though fortunately in such a feeble voice that it was more like a mouse's squeak than anything else. Of the two of us, it was I who was in the worse plight, and I shall never forget how tirelessly Tilda worked to put me to rights. She packed me up in clean rags soaked in cold water to stop the bleeding, made me some tea, and later on, when I felt faint, crept downstairs to the butler's pantry and stole some brandy out of Valentine's private bottle to revive me. She changed the linen on my bed, hid the soiled sheets up the chimney until such time as we were able to destroy them, and put her own on my bed, vowing that she could sleep very well in blankets until she could smuggle up an extra pair from the linen room. Luckily there were so many odd sheets lying round waiting to be mended, that it would not be difficult to get hold of a couple when the rest of the staff were out of the way.

When she had made me comfortable, she laid the baby in the crook of my arm, and we both pored adoringly over him.

'Rum little card,' said Tilda with a chuckle. 'Got a head of hair on him already, see? More'n most babies have.' She ruffled up the soft lock of brown hair on the top of his tiny skull. 'Well, Skivvy, you've got him! You and my lady have been running neck to neck, and you've got in first!'

I laid my cheek against the tiny warm head. For the moment I was too happy to think of anything but that I had a baby, a son of my own. I listened to his breathing, faint but regular, against my heart, and knew that I loved him more than anything on earth and always would—my little son. It was odd that neither then, nor ever, did I think of Valentine in connection with him. He was always all my own. My very own!

Tilda looked down on us both with pardonable pride.

'I've done a good job for you and your brat, Skivvy,' she said. 'Lucky I know plenty about it, ain't it? You might easily have lost him, coming so early, if I hadn't had my wits about me. You'll have to lie up a day or so, you know, or maybe the bleeding will start again. We'll have to think up some sort of story about your being ill.'

'What shall I do if anyone comes up to look after me?' I said. 'We'll have to hide him somewhere—and if he should start to cry. . . .'

'Don't worry,' Tilda told me. 'I'll say you've got a spotty sort of rash and maybe it's

70

measles. There's a lot down in the village, and the others will be only too glad to leave you to me, 'cos I've had 'em. You'll be all right for a day or two, Skivvy—but what on earth are you going to do with him? Where can he go?'

Panic seized me and I held the baby close.

'I—I don't know,' I said helplessly.

'Well, for the present he'll have to stay here,' Tilda said. 'I'll dig a place for him in my trunk, and prop the lid open so's he can breathe.'

'No,' I said. 'No, Tilda! You'd likely forget and slam the lid down and he'd die. There's that big cardboard hat-box—I'll make a cradle for him out of that and punch plenty of breathing holes in it, and then if anyone should come up here all they'd see would be just another box. But what shall we do if he cries? I suppose he will—all babies cry.'

'We'll have to stop that, at all costs,' Tilda said firmly. 'I'll get my sister to send us a bottle of the sleeping stuff she uses to keep her brats quiet at night. Give them a drop in their milk and nothing'll wake 'em. It's grand stuff.'

I felt doubtful about this. I'd heard stories about babies being made ill or even dying through being given sleeping stuff by their nurses. But I didn't say anything. Between us

71

we made up a bed for my little one in the cardboard box, making a soft mattress for him out of one of my nightgowns and all the soft, clean oddments we could find. I covered him up with a red flannel petticoat of mine, and Tilda, having punched plenty of good-sized holes in the box lid, carried him over to the far corner, where there was a collection of boxes and other things, and left him there to sleep. Then we slept ourselves until dawn.

Tilda's ruse about the measles worked admirably. Measles was still regarded then as a childish complaint for which it was hardly worth calling in the doctor. But nobody wanted to catch it, and no-one except Tilda, who had already had it, was allowed to come near me—more especially as lo and behold, while I was having my baby, my lady had been going through the same ordeal, and when Tilda went down in the morning she found that the longed-for son had arrived! Though his was not a premature birth like my child's; she had conceived two months before I had.

Despite being an early bird—Tilda and I called him Birdie because of this—my baby thrived. During the four days which were all the 'leave' I dared allow myself, I could see what good progress he was making. I tried to feed him myself, but my milk was scanty for some reason, perhaps because of my youth. But thanks to my farm training I was able to feed him as I had used to feed lambs that lost their mothers, by dipping my finger in milk and letting him suck it, and so gradually training him to take a bottle.

Tilda went over to a sister of hers who lived not far away and had several children, including one very young one, and brought back a feeding-bottle, together with a bottle of the sleeping stuff that was said to keep babies quiet. Heavens know what story she told her! I never asked. It was a flat brown bottle, and when it was opened it smelt rather sickly, but the stuff did its work all right. Birdie wasn't a crying baby, but from time to time he made noises that might have attracted attention if anybody had been near to hear, and I didn't dare to take any risks. So I was obliged to dose him, and certainly it did not seem to do him any harm.

It only took me a few days to get back to my normal health, for I was young and strong and, anyway, in those days, women in my walk of life didn't make much fuss about having babies. As soon as I was well enough, Tilda spread the news that my rash hadn't been measles after all. Just an ordinary rash 'brought on by eating too much,' was Mrs. Dibben's acid comment. I came downstairs and took up my ordinary life again, thankful that so much sewing had accumulated during my absence that I was able to sit down doing it for most of the day. People greeted my recovery kindly enough, but everyone was still so excited about the new Stilwell baby that interest in me was a very minor affair.

There was a new member of the household now—a nurse for the baby heir. She was a good-looking, dark young woman with a figure that immediately attracted the attention of Valentine. Mrs. Beck had been given leave to go and look after a dying sister, so Valentine was able to amuse himself freely with the new attraction. The nurse, whose name was Phemie Harold, was by no means unresponsive, and the staff was watching the development of the affair with great interest.

I myself was not in the least interested. I seemed to have forgotten all about Valentine. My whole attention was taken up with the miracle that had happened to me, the miracle of having a child. But my wonder and delight were shot through with fear. What *was* I to do with him? Where could I go? What chance had I of finding employment, burdened with a bastard child?

74

Tilda, who from the first had assumed that the child was Johnny's, had taken it for granted that we would now get married. She was astonished when, in a moment of exasperation with her badgering me to speak to him, I told her that the baby wasn't Johnny's at all. I refused to tell her whose it was, though. Instead of being shocked, she chuckled and looked at me with something like admiration in her eyes.

'*You* of all people! I'd never have thought it of you! You're a deep one—and all the boys say you're so stand-offish! And now this!' She begged me to tell her the name of my lover and how and when it had all begun, but I wouldn't discuss it, and at last she desisted from teasing me about that and turned to urging me to marry Johnny as soon as possible, then, when we were safely married, to spring the baby upon him. He was so besotted on me, she said, that likely he'd take it and bring it up as his own once he'd got over the shock. What a fool I'd been, she said, not to sleep with him as well as with my mysterious lover. For then the child could have been fathered on Johnny and he'd never have known it wasn't his.

I told her angrily that, whatever I was, I wasn't *that* sort of girl—to sleep with two lovers at a time. And I would never consider making use of Johnny in that shabby way. Somehow, I told her, I would find a way of getting my baby cared for until I was in a position to look after him myself. But even as I spoke I knew well enough what difficulties faced me. Even to-day the path of a working girl with an illegitimate child is hard enough—in those days there wasn't an earthly chance of my getting a job in any decent house if there was the smallest suspicion of my having a child in the background—let alone bringing it with me.

I would look down on the face of my sleeping baby and think bitterly how much less lucky he was than that other baby, born in the same house on the same day. Little Frederick, the future Lord Stilwell, would be lapped in luxury from the beginning to the end of his life. Surrounded by adoring relatives, by servants eager to do his bidding, with money enough to fulfil his every wish—it wasn't fair! It wasn't fair that one should have so much and the other so little!

This bitterness worked like leaven within me after I had my first glimpse of the little heir. I ventured to ask the new nurse if I might be allowed a peep at the baby. My lady had always been so kind to me, I told her, that

I was sure she would say yes if she was asked. Nurse Harold shrugged her shoulders and said she'd ask her, and that very afternoon she told me that my lady would like me to go to her room and she'd show me the baby herself.

Nurse ushered me into the beautiful bedroom, and on tip-toe I ventured up to my lady's big bed. She looked very white and frail, but the happy light in her eyes made her look lovelier than ever. Her room was full of flowers, and her bedside table was stacked with piles of letters and telegrams—of congratulations, I suppose.

And beside the bed was a great cradle of carved oak on rockers—I'd never seen such an elaborate cradle before, though, of course, I'd seen many ordinary rocking-cradles in the cottages near my home.

My lady saw my eyes on it and smiled.

'It's not the fashion now, I know, to use these cradles,' she said. 'The fashionable ones are made of basket work and trimmed with muslin and ribbons—so pretty! I would have liked one of those, but it seems that it is unlucky for the heir of the Stilwells to be laid in anything but this ancient family affair! I'm glad you're well again, Emily, and that it was only a summer rash and not measles. Had it been measles, it would have been weeks before you could have come near my treasure. Look. Isn't he lovely?'

I gazed down silently at the little creature nestled in the pile of soft white blankets in the great carved cradle. He was a little thing, no bigger than my own baby though he was a full-time child and mine had come two months too soon. He was startlingly like my son to look at, too, with the same coloured soft brown hair on his little head. As I stared at him, a wave of fierce envy struck me like a blow. What had my son done that he should be born to a life of fear and hardship, while this woman's child would have such great possessions, such luxury and ease? So bitter did I feel that it was as much as I could do to murmur a few conventional words about how beautiful he was, how glad we all were that he had come at last, and how I hoped my lady had not had too bad a time.

When at length I thanked my lady for letting me see the baby and left the room, I rushed upstairs to my attic, and flinging myself on the bed gave way to a storm of hysterical tears. Tilda looked curiously at my reddened eyes when I went down to tea, and I saw Johnny gazing anxiously at me several times during the meal. Fearing that he might come after me to the linen room, after tea was finished I took a pile of my sewing and went along to a room in a distant wing of the house which was very seldom used. The room was only sparsely furnished—just a bed and a table and a chair or two. I knew of it because Mr. Valentine had taken me there once or twice after Tilda had come back from her holiday and it was no longer safe for him to come to my room. I thought I would have it to myself at this hour of the day, and be safe from any possible visit from Johnny. But as I went along the passage towards it, I saw that the door was half-open and I heard a murmur of voices from within—Valentine's and the new nurse's. I paused and listened, and heard Valentine say:

'In this room we'd be as snug as a bug in a rug, as the saying is, Miss Harold. Why not slip along for a chat to-night when the folks are all abed? I'll bring up a bottle of wine and some glasses—oh, come on, now! Say yes! It's years since I took to a girl as I've taken to you.'

I stole silently forward and peeped into the room. They were standing together by the window, and as I looked his arm slid round her waist and he pulled her close to him.

'Come on, kiss me!' he said, and for a full

minute they clung together, exchanging kisses with the ardour of experts at the love game.

'Make it to-night?' he begged.

The nurse drew away from him, adjusting her cap with a demure pretence of bashfulness.

'Oh, Mr. Valentine, you are a one! How can I—with the baby to keep an eye upon and my lady, too?' she said.

'Well, you've been away a couple of hours this afternoon, haven't you?' he said impatiently.

'That's allowed. I'm entitled to two hours' rest and recreation every day. The housemaid sat with my lady while I was out.'

'You don't have to sit in my lady's room all night, do you?'

'Oh, no! She takes stuff to sleep at night, and the baby's moved into my lord's dressing-room which opens out of her room, and I sleep on the day bed that's there.'

'Does my lady sleep sound? Really sound?' he asked.

'She does when she's taken her sleeping-draught. When she's taken that, you couldn't wake her for hours even if you tried.'

'Well then, it's easy,' he laughed that bark of a laugh of his. 'You give her an extra strong dose to make sure, and give the brat some of it, too, to keep him quiet as well. Then when they're both asleep and the house is quiet, you come along here, my girl, and I'll show you some love-making that you'll never forget!'

CHAPTER SIX

LORD STILWELL'S HEIR

I TOLD Tilda what I had overheard, and she chortled with amusement. To find that the haughty nurse, brought in at great expense to look after Lady Stilwell and the baby heir, who had turned up her nose at us as being mere servant girls, shared the weakness of any one of us, seemed to Tilda one of the best jokes she had heard for a long time.

Seeing Lady Stilwell and hearing her kind voice again had revived all my old love for her. I visualized her waking, despite the sleeping-draught, in Phemie Harold's absence, and needing something and calling out in vain. So I determined not to undress that night but, instead, to slip downstairs and keep a watch on Valentine's love nest—which I could do easily from the depth of a big cupboard set in the wall close by the door—and when Nurse Harold kept the appointment, if she did, go back and steal quietly into my lord's dressing-room, where I would sit keeping watch until the wanderer got tired of love-making and came back to her neglected duties. The dressing-room had a door leading out into the corridor, as well as the one connecting with my lady's room, so it would be quite simple to get into it without running any risk of waking my lady. Nurse would be furious, of course, to find me there, but she would not dare to say anything since to complain would be to admit that she had left her charges unattended.

I told Tilda what I meant to do, as I had to get someone to watch over my son while I was away—between us we had somehow managed to space out our duties so that one or the other of us had a look at him every hour, more or less. Tilda thought I was mad to lose half a night's sleep over such a matter, and said that the only thing that might make it worthwhile would be the expression on Nurse Harold's face when she came back and found me there! But she promised to watch over Birdie while I was away, and after supper that night I carried out my plan. I could tell from the sounds downstairs when my lord had gone to his bedroom, setting Valentine free to retire himself, and I slipped into a cupboard in the corridor close to Valentine's 'love nest,' and waited for the love birds to appear.

Yes! There they were! Whispering and giggling together they came down the passage, went into the little room and shut the door. I waited a moment, then I crept out of my hiding-place and fled through the long corridor and down the main stair-case to the first floor, where my lord and lady had their bedrooms. The dressing-room door was ajar, so I pushed it open and went in. There was a bed set along one wall, turned down all ready to be occupied; and beside it was the oak cradle, its tiny occupant all but hidden in a nest of fleecy coverings.

I tiptoed across to the further door and peeped into my lady's room. She was lying on her side, facing me, sound asleep, looking so young and innocent as she lay there that it was difficult to believe she was the mother of a big girl like Miss Angela. She was so sound asleep that I believe I could have touched her without awaking her, but, of course, I didn't, and I went back into the dressing-room, pulled out a purple spencer I was knitting for my grandmother, and sitting down in a low chair near the cradle began to knit steadily. While I knitted, in the soft yellow light of an oil lamp, I went back again and again to the terrible problem facing me—what *was* I to do about Birdie?

I could not keep him hidden indefinitely in the cardboard box. It was getting on for a week now since he was born, and so far my secret was still undiscovered. But I knew that could not go on much longer, and I wondered, tremblingly, what on earth I could say or do when it all came out. In my mind's eye I saw the shocked faces of my friends among the staff, and my lady's reproachful eyes. I could almost hear her say: 'Oh, Emily! And you so carefully brought up!' With an impatient gesture I tried to put the troubling thoughts out of my head, accidentally my hand struck the carved hood of the cradle and set it rocking. Fearing lest I might have awakened the baby, I peered into the cradle—then I started back in astonished alarm. For the baby in its nest of pink blankets looked so pale. So terribly waxen white—like a dead thing!

I touched the little body—and it was cold. The stony cold of a dead creature! Unable to believe it, I bent over it and felt for a heart-beat. But there was none. The unbelievable was true—the child was dead! Dead after a bare five days of life—the longed-for son and heir of the Stilwells. My heart swelled with horrified pity for my lady lying so innocently asleep in the next room, all unconscious of the shattering blow that awaited her when she awoke.

I was so dumbfounded that for several minutes I must have sat there, staring. What *could* have caused this tragic death? The baby had looked healthy enough when I saw it last, and I had not heard that it ailed at all. Then I remembered Valentine's callous words: 'Give her an extra strong dose to make sure, and give the brat some of it, too,' and I realized what had happened. That evil nurse had given mother and child extra strong doses of the sleeping-draught so that she could spend an hour or two with Valentine! Whatever the stuff was it did not harm my lady—though I heard that she slept very late the following morning. But plainly it was too strong for the baby, who had died quietly—probably very soon after the fatal dose since he was already cold.

Then, as I sat there staring, an idea struck me like a blinding light. Here, before me, was the solution of problem. The two babies had been born on the same day and were astonishingly alike in size and appearance. I had been struck by their similarity the first time I saw the little heir. Both were fair-skinned and blue-eyed with soft, silky light-brown hair. There was no mark such as a mole or anything like that on my Birdie's little body. Was there one on this pitiful little mite? I forced myself to strip the clothes from the little dead thing, and looked it over carefully from head to foot. Yes, it was free from any blemish. Here was the answer to my trouble, if only I had the courage to do it! I could steal upstairs with the dead child in my arms, hidden in the folds of my knitting, bring down my son and put him in this baby's place.

Changed at birth! Yes, it was a plot worthy of an early Victorian melodrama—but it held for me the promise of two vital things. It meant salvation for me—freedom from the awful fate of having to carry the burden of my folly around with me, to render me unfit for wifehood and spoil my chances in life. And for Birdie? For Birdie it would mean salvation also. He would step clean into the life I would have given worlds to present him with myself. A life of comfort and security—a life in which he would find opportunity to travel, meet influential folk, learn to ride, to dance, to shoot, to do any and everything a normal young man longs to do! All this lay now in my hands to give him, could I but find the courage to carry it out.

I thrust behind me the knowledge that all my life thence-forward would be haunted by the memory of a little warm body nestled against me, a sleepy smile, a pair of eyes as blue as the turquoises in my lady's favourite necklace. I dare not let myself think of that in that moment. Swiftly I gathered up the poor little cold body and the clothes I had stripped it of, and wrapping it up in the folds of my knitting I slipped out of the room, and ran like a hare down the empty corridors and up the stairs to my attic. Tilda, I was thankful to find, wasn't there—she was carrying on a violent flirtation at the time with one of the grooms, and doubtless she was out in the grounds with him somewhere, unknown to Mrs. Beck and the elder servants. As I drew Birdie out of his own warm nest into my arms, my heart all but failed me. He was so warm and sweet and tiny—how *could* I let him go? But I set my lips and went grimly on with my task of dressing him in the dead baby's clothes. I kept before my mind's eye as I did so, the lovely, happy face of my lady as she showed me her child. Besides giving my son a wonderful life and a wonderful mother—I would also, though all unknown, be giving my lady back her dream—the son for whom she had longed.

When at last my baby was dressed and the little dead body hidden in the hatbox, I clutched my precious bundle to my breast and went swiftly down the stairs. As I started to descend them, I thought I caught a glimpse of Tilda stepping into the corridor from the fire-escape, returning from her rendezvous, but I did not stop to make sure. Speed was everything—and down the stairs I went, and a few moments later Birdie was tucked up inside the soft blankets in the Stilwell cradle.

I looked down at him critically when I had settled him comfortably. Would anyone suspect that the Stilwell child had gone and left a changeling in his place? I did not think it likely. If they are of the same size and colouring, young babies of the same age are amazingly alike. Lady Stilwell did not really see a great deal of her child. Even when he was in her room, he was asleep in his cradle most of the time. The chief danger was Nurse Harold. It was she who had most to do with him. If she was very observant, it was possible that she might notice some difference.

Even as I thought of her, I heard her step outside. She entered the room, then stopped dead when she saw me and scowled. I had no wish to antagonize her, so I spoke apologetically before she could say anything.

'I brought down some mending I'd done for my lady, Nurse,' I said, as calmly as I could. 'As I found you weren't here, I couldn't resist the chance to have a peep at the baby.'

She looked at me sideways—like a cat that can't make up its mind whether to scratch or be friendly.

'I'd only been gone for a minute,' she said acidly at last.

Liar! thought I, who knew she had been away for a good hour and a half. But I said as sweet as honey:

'Oh, yes, of course. I do hope you don't mind. But downstairs we don't often get a chance to see the son and heir. He's a bonny baby, isn't he?'

I had to say it—I had to know my fate at once. When she looked at him, would she see any difference? There was only a little bit of his face showing above the bedclothes, and I bent down and pulled them aside so that my Birdie's whole head was exposed. The nurse came and stood beside me and looked down into the cradle.

'He's the usual sort of baby,' she allowed, gazing at him critically. 'Nice healthy brat, lucky little devil! Heir to all this estate, just fancy! Some children have all the luck! You're the one they call "Skivvy," aren't you? What a name! Don't you hate it?'

I shrugged my shoulders and moved towards the door. I was satisfied. She suspected nothing. Now I had to get away quickly, for my knees were shaking, and tears of bitter anguish were smarting behind my lashes. It was all I could do to answer her question, and my voice sounded hoarse and queer as I spoke.

'I'm used to it now. You see, my name's Skeffington, so it came sort of pat. It would seem odd now if they called me anything else. Good night.'

The nurse echoed my good night—and never knew that it was not to her that I said it, but to my darling son.

*   *   *

We buried the little cold body of Lord Stilwell's heir, Tilda and me, the next day, in the heart of the great shrubbery of rhododendrons, syringa, and other massed bushes, that formed a belt of flowering shrubs down one side of the grounds, not far from the Manor house. It was inevitable that Tilda should find out what I had done. In a vague kind of way, I had hoped that when she saw the dead baby in the hatbox she would conclude that it was Birdie who had died, in the sudden mysterious way babies do sometimes die in the very early days of their life. But Tilda was too quick in the uptake, as they say, to think that. It was she I had seen climbing into the passage from the fire-escape as I fled down the stairs, and she had observed that I had a baby in my arms. Curiosity had taken her at once to the hat-box and she had not been slow to guess what had taken place. She was waiting for me when I walked unsteadily into the attic room I shared with her.

'Poor old Skivvy!' she said, and her voice was kind. 'I'm sorry for you. I know when you've had a brat it's hard to part from it. My sister Martha had to give away her first. 'Twas born out of wedlock and she couldn't keep it, nor Mother neither, and she got it adopted. She cried and moped for months after it had gone, though it wasn't more'n a few weeks old. Here, I've made some tea, you'd better have some. Then you can tell me what happened to the Stilwell kid.'

I sipped the hot tea and felt better.

'Then you know what I've done?' I asked dully. 'I found the Stilwell baby dead in the cradle—poisoned by that nurse's sleep-ing-stuff, I guess. And I suddenly realized—'

Tilda finished the sentence for me.

'Realized what a chance had fallen into your lap! Well, I don't blame you! It's what I'd have done myself if I'd been in your place. It's the best thing that could have happened really, Skivvy. Now Birdie's got a fine father and mother, and a rich life you couldn't ever have given him. My lady's heart won't be broken, and you've got a weight rolled off your shoulders that looked like hanging on and holding you back all your life. We'll do something to-morrow about hiding this poor little wretch, and then all you've got to do will be to try and forget it all.'

Good advice, no doubt—but, alas, the one thing I could not do!

The burial of the tiny body was the easiest thing in the world as it turned out. I carried it downstairs in the morning, hidden beneath a pile of mending in my sewing basket and put it behind the drawing-room door. I was the first maid down, except for Biddy, who had already lighted the kitchen fire, and when I had put the kettle on for Mrs. Dibben's early tea, I slipped back and took up my basket and carried it out through the french windows of the drawing-room, which opened on to the terrace. At the back of the house, the stable hands were already up and about their work, but here in the front all was quiet, with the blinds still drawn in all the windows. I stole quietly along the terrace and left the basket hidden deep in the shrubbery, in the centre of a thick, bushy, rhododrendon. Then, unseen, I went back to the house, made the tea, and carried the tray to Mrs. Dibben.

Later that day, when things were quiet, Tilda and I crept into the shrubbery from the farther side and buried the poor little body, that had known but a brief five days of life, in the soft, black earth at the roots of the flower-laden tree.

We both cried a little as we worked, for it seemed so pitiful, and I said a prayer as we dug, me with a trowel and Tilda with an old children's spade with a broken handle which she had found somewhere. I had wrapped the baby in my best nightgown—I had a queer feeling that somehow I was giving him *something* at least—and we buried him in it, and a few purple petals from the flowers clustered over his head fell on him softly as we put back the earth. When we had finished the little grave, we parted, I went in one direction and Tilda in another, for we did not want to be seen together lest anyone should be curious as to what we were doing in that part of the garden. I emerged boldly from the front of the shrubbery, carrying an armful of syringa blossoms which I knew my lady loved, so I had my answer pat if anyone questioned me. And Tilda slipped out on the other side and went back to the house by way of the kitchen garden and the greenhouses. If anyone had seen her they would never have asked what *she* was doing—they all knew Tilda too well to wonder about that. They would just have concluded that she had sneaked out for a brief flirtation with one of the men.

For several days I lived on tenterhooks, wondering whether the baby would be recognized for what he was—a changeling. My ears were on the stretch, waiting to hear the cry: 'Why, it's a strange baby! It's not Master Frederick at all!' But the cry never came, and at last I realized that I had succeeded in what I had set out to do. I had managed to substitute my own living baby for the dead Stilwell child, and he was now and for all time the Honourable Frederick Stilwell, later to be Lord Stilwell, owner of the Manor, a house in town, a shooting-box in Scotland, a vast stretch of property besides. And I—I was free once more.

Free. Yet more wretchedly unhappy than I had ever imagined that anybody could be. I had only known my baby for a few brief days, yet during that time he had wound himself so completely about my heart that the thought of him was with me night and day. I could not rid myself of the longing for him. I used to wake at nights with a start, feeling his warm little body against me—and feel my heart sink like a stone when I realized that it was only a dream. In my ears I seemed to hear the little cooing sigh he would give as his downy head nestled into the hollow of my shoulder, and I could feel the touch of his curling fingers that clung to my own. Oh! There are no words in which to describe how I hungered and anguished for him—my own child, my pretty son, the baby I had brought into the world!

I took to making excuses to go to my lady's room, simply in order to catch a glimpse of Birdie, and when—as happened once or twice—I found him cuddled into her arms, such a storm of furious jealousy shook me that I was alarmed, and had to turn my head away quickly and busy myself pretending to look for something or other that needed mending, for fear lest I should show my feelings in my face. My preoccupation with the new baby was noticed with interest by the staff. I was teased about it, and told that I ought to get married and have a baby of my own since I was so fond of them, until Tilda took fright and warned me that it looked odd that I should show such an interest in the child.

'If you can't keep away from him,' she said bluntly one night when we were up in our attic, 'if you can't keep away from him, then you'd better take yourself off and be safe.'

'Take myself off?' I repeated. 'Do you mean leave the Manor?'

'Yes—why not? It's asking for trouble, to keep on hanging round that blessed child the way you're doing. And there's another thing. That Valentine is sniffing around you again. Oh, you needn't open your eyes at me—I know it was him, right enough. I can put two and two together as well as most folk, and though you had me guessing for a time, you've let slip one or two things which put me on the track at last. I'm right, aren't I?'

I nodded forlornly, and she continued:

'Now you do one of two things. You can either leave and get another place, which won't be difficult, for you're a good all-round maid and my lady's sure to give you a fine reference. Or you can marry Johnny! He's got the offer of a good job as coachman to a lady in London, and he wants to take it. Only he wants you, too, and he's afraid you'll turn him down.'

With a sudden guilty feeling, I remembered Johnny. I had been so wrapped up in my own misery the past few weeks that I had barely noticed his constant, kindly presence, and I looked at Tilda now with attention.

'Well,' I said slowly. 'Maybe you're right,

Tilda. I'm beginning to realize that I shall *have* to leave here, or I shall give myself away somehow. But yet how can I go away and leave him?'

'Don't be a fool!' said Tilda brusquely. 'You've left him already, haven't you? He's not yours any more—he's the Stilwell's. You can't alter what you've done. For goodness sake, do it completely and make a clean cut! It'll be safer for you and me and everybody in the end.'

I thought it over and over again, and at last I promised to marry Johnny. And one of the memories in my life that I like best to linger on now, is the memory of my last scene with Valentine. Tilda was right. After the monthly nurse had left and been replaced by a plump, comfortable, elderly Nannie, he had begun to cast eyes in my direction again. One evening, when Mrs. Dibben had gone to bed and I was alone in the kitchen, he strolled in with his hands in his pockets. Leaning against the kitchen table he surveyed me with the cool appraising look I knew so well.

'So you managed to get rid of the encumbrance, Emmie?' he remarked. 'I congratulate you—both on that and on getting back your figure as well. It's better than ever, by jove!'

I went on with my job of tidying up the kitchen, as I said brusquely:

'Don't waste your compliments on me. Keep 'em for Mrs. Beck.'

'Oh, she's all right,' he said. 'Gave in her notice at Easter and is getting her trousseau ready. All in a flutter, the old fool, as though she was as young as you. Almost as fluttery as you were, Emmie. Remember?'

'There's nothing about it I want to remember,' I told him. 'It's over and done with, and I don't care if I never see or hear of you again!'

He grinned.

'Ah, but you're going to see me,' he said. 'We're not getting married until the autumn, and until then I shall be here. What about meeting me somewhere to-night? Beck goes to bed early, and I shall be free then. What about it?'

I swung round to face him.

'If you're free, *I'm* not!' I snapped at his grinning face. 'I'm through with you for good and all. And in a month I'm going to marry Johnny Bligh.'

NOTE BY SALLIE STILWELL

Here there came a big gap in the story, and
99

when Eve and I were trying to piece it together we often had great difficulty in finding
the next section and had to fill in the vacuum
as best we could. It was fascinating work,
though, and gave Eve and me an absorbing
job to do in the long winter evenings when
Eve wasn't broadcasting. We told one or two
of our friends about it, and one night Eve read
some of it aloud to one of them—a publisher's
reader who had dropped into the flat for a
glass of beer. He listened with interest, and at
length he said:

'Why don't you put it into readable order
and send it along to my firm? Sounds to me as
though you might have a best-seller on your
hands—"Life Story of a Victorian Servant
Girl."'

Eve and I looked at each other.

'I never thought—' we both began.

'Well, start thinking now, and get to work
on it. From the state it's in it won't be an easy
job, but it sounds to me as though it would be
worth doing.' He looked at me. 'You can type,
Sallie, can't you?'

I nodded and he went on: 'Well, when
you've sorted it out, type it out properly and
let me have a look at it.'

That's what really started us making a
book of it. It took us months before we were

able to write "Finis" at the end of Emily Skeffington's life story. But finish it we did at last, and made a fairly coherent thing of it, too. As we went along, we discovered how it was she was able to write so well. That had puzzled us at first, knowing the kind of education that was all village children could expect in the 1870's. But I'm not going to spoil the story by anticipating events—how it happened will come along in its proper time.

As I have said, there was a gap when we reached the point recorded in the above chapter. When we were able to decipher the script again, Skivvy was married, and was living in a flat over the stables in a mews off Bryanston Square where Mr. and Mrs. Fortescue, Johnny's new employers, had a big house. Skivvy's grandmother had died, presumably of a stroke, and she herself had had a little girl who only survived her birth for a little while.

As far as we could tell, Skivvy and her Johnny were pretty happy together. But it was plain that Skivvy was still fretting for her baby boy, who, when her story became readable again, must have been about three years old.

CHAPTER SEVEN

LONDON DAYS

IT TOOK a long time for me, born and brought up in the quiet of the country, to get used to the noise of the traffic in London. The swirling procession of jingling hansoms and four-wheelers, of buses—drawn by horses then, of course—of delivery vans and a dozen others, terrified me, and I would stand for ages on the kerb of the pavement before I dared to cross a street, even when the policeman on duty held up the traffic for me, as sometimes happened. And the dust and dirt that drifted into our little three-roomed flat over the coach-house in the mews behind the tall houses in Bryanston Square worried me almost to weeping! Try as I might, I never was able to keep the place as clean and sweet as I wanted it. When I looked at my carefully-washed lace curtains grown dingy after only having been up a week or two, I felt glad, for the first time, that my dear old grandmother was dead and couldn't see them. She would have read me a lecture to beat all lectures on keeping up the standard of cleanliness she'd taught me if she had ever seen them!

When I began to get accustomed to the noise and dirt, though, there were certain things about London that I couldn't help liking. The shops were simply wonderful. I never tired of gaping in the windows crowded with beautiful things to buy. And I liked going to Hyde Park on a fine Sunday in spring or summer, to watch the Church Parade of smart people promenading up and down on the long walk under the trees, between Stanhope Gate and the big bronze statue put up in memory of the Duke of Wellington. I'd never before seen such an array of smart ladies, and though now people laugh at the fashions of that day, to my mind they were so wonderful that even a plain lady couldn't help looking well in them.

I saw quite a lot of the gentry and the way they behaved, for Mrs. Fortescue had a calling day when other ladies, and sometimes gentlemen, too, used to come calling, and I used to go in as an extra maid to help serve the teas. Mr. and Mrs. Fortescue weren't as high up in Society as Lord and Lady Stilwell, because Mr. Fortescue was in the City, and though that wasn't as bad as being in trade, it meant that he wasn't such a gentleman as my lord. But he was very rich, and his wife had been the daughter of a knight which helped a lot, and they had invitations to a lot of houses where, as Mrs. Henham, the cook, said, they would never have been let through the door twenty years earlier. Society wasn't what it was, getting altogether too mixed, Mrs. Henham said!

But Mrs. Fortescue had been determined to get her husband accepted by the right people, and she had made her relations pull all the strings they could to get him elected to the right clubs and the right parties, and by the time Johnny and I worked for her, she seemed to have succeeded in getting him where she wanted. Her eldest daughter, Miss Beryl, had been presented at Court and was engaged to a young gentleman who was private secretary to somebody very important in Parliament, and the second daughter, Miss Sybil, was to be presented, too, when she was old enough. A big ball was to be given for her coming out when she was eighteen, and she was for ever talking about this ball, what she would wear for it, and all that. Beside the two daughters, the Fortescues had one son, Mr. Arnold, who was at Oxford studying for a degree—though as far as I could gather from the talk below stairs, all he was really doing was writing home continually for more money and drinking a lot more than was good for him.

I never grew fond of Mrs. Fortescue like I was fond of my lady—I was fond of my lady, I think, in a different sort of way from anybody else. But I liked her and the family well enough, and once I got used to it the exciting London life they lived, in which to a limited extent I took part, kept me interested and amused. The first summer Johnny worked for them was a long and sunny one, and when I wasn't wanted to help in the house I used to go out a lot in the afternoons to the park to watch the people. I saw the famous Mrs. Langtry several times, always with a crowd of gentlemen around her. She was a lady friend of the Prince of Wales, and I saw him, too, once or twice. I used to enjoy those outings very much, and I loved the music halls where Johnny would take me on his evenings off. His evenings off weren't so frequent as they had been at the Manor, for the Fortescues went out a good deal and Johnny was needed to drive them most nights. But when he did get a free evening we made the most of it, and we used to enjoy ourselves no end.

Yes, I settled well into London life after a while, and but for the grief and shock of losing our baby girl we were very happy

105

Johnny and I. That is, *he* was very happy, and I was happy when I could put a certain thought out of my mind—the thought of a little boy who was growing up without me. Unfortunately for me, I could never thrust that thought away for very long. I had hoped that when I was living a new life in a new place—and especially when I was pregnant with my poor little girl who died—that my aching hunger for Birdie would fade. But it never did. I kept on remembering how he looked the last sight I had of him, snuggled among the blankets of the great oak cradle which had sheltered so many of the Stilwell heirs and now held a changeling—the child of a little serving maid called Emmie Skeffington. I could see his dimpled face, eyes closed in sleep, puckered mouth pouting as though for a kiss—and it was as if a knife twisted in my heart, and I wanted to rush off to the Manor and snatch my baby and run away with him to the end of the world! When this mood took me I was glum and wretched, and it used to worry Johnny dreadfully. He would watch me wistfully and ask what was wrong and if he had done anything to upset me, and what could he do to get me smiling again. He told me that my smile was one of the things he loved me best for. He said it was a sunny smile that lighted up everything for him—quite poetic he was at times, my Johnny, and that used to touch me deeply. But, of course, he was the last person in whom I could ever confide.

I missed Tilda badly for a time. She was the only person who knew my secret and with whom I could have talked about my pain. Her cheery commonsense, her ready laughter, even her tendency to bawdy jokes, had meant more to me than I had realized. But Tilda had left the Manor, run off with one of the men, a married one, and my lord and lady were very angry and were looking after the deserted wife, left, poor girl, with a young baby and no money at all. Mrs. Dibben, to whom I wrote from time to time—for I simply *had* to hear occasionally how my baby was getting on, and she usually made some mention of the 'heir' when she answered my letters—told me that among other bits of news. Much as I liked Tilda, and much as I owed her, I could not but feel shocked when I heard what she had done. But that was Tilda all over. If she wanted anything, a man or anything else, she must have it, no matter what.

In my letters to Mrs. Dibben I never failed to ask after my lady and the little boy, and if a letter came from her in which there was no mention of either, my day was spoilt, and I would be gloomy and depressed for hours, so that poor Johnny would be puzzled and unhappy until I recovered my spirits. But actually she rarely forgot to reply to my questions, for she was keenly interested herself in the baby's progress, and thanks to her I learnt when he took his first stumbling steps, when he began to talk, when his hair was first cut— she sent me a lock of it, and I have it still— and how he looked, and laughed, and played. I read and treasured every word she wrote about him, even though reading it twisted the knife in my aching heart.

* * *

Lord and Lady Stilwell always came up to town, when my lady was well, to their house in Chesham Square for the season, and when my baby was two years old they began bringing him with them, Mrs. Dibben told me, for they could not bear to be parted from him for long. The temptation to go and see if I could catch sight of my darling was strong, but I wanted to see him myself unseen if that were possible, and I did not see how I could manage it. So for two years I stifled my longing, and then one day Johnny told me that he had run

108

into William, one of the footmen, having a drink in a public house nearby, and William had asked after me and invited us both to come and visit them all. It was impossible to refuse without looking churlish, and, as things fell out, I was actually able to see and to talk to my darling! Not for long, and, alas, not alone—but perhaps that was as well, for the temptation to put my arms round him and kiss him and cry over him might have overcome me, and he would have been frightened, poor sweet.

We went to Chesham Square one sunny afternoon in May, and the beds in the Square gardens were all ablaze with colour and the air sweet with scent. I'd put my best things on to do Johnny credit, a brown costume and a brown straw hat with a tuft of nasturtiums in the front and a little metal ornament, a winged beetle, stuck among the flowers. I think I looked nice, but my heart was beating like a trip-hammer as we went down the area steps and into the corridor that led to the kitchen and the servants' hall at the far end. Mrs. Dibben was waiting for us, and Biddy was there, grown into quite a pretty girl, and Jane, and one or two of the others. The new butler, Mr. Dowden—Valentine and Mrs. Beck had married and left long ago—greeted us pleasantly, and we all sat down to tea. For Johnny's sake I exerted myself to be gay, though all the time there was something tugging at my heartstrings—if only I could see him for a minute! Just for a minute—that was all! And then William and Edgar, who had been serving tea upstairs, came down and after greeting us Edgar said:

'By the way, my lady saw you coming along. She was standing in the window and want to see you both. Specially you, Skivvy.'

I was so staggered at this sudden answer to my silent prayer that, for the moment, I had no words, and after he had helped himself to a buttered crumpet, Edgar went on:

'She wants you to see the baby—though he's not a baby now, and mind you don't tell him I called him that! Their visitors have gone, so when you've done your tea, Skivvy, you go on up and make your bob to your betters.'

Johnny was shy and wouldn't come with me, so I went upstairs alone. I knocked softly on the drawing-room door, and a thrill ran through me as my lady's sweet voice called:

'Is that Emily? Come in, Emily. I am so glad to see you.'

I went in, and there she was, smiling at me with her old charming, friendly smile—my dear lady. And playing on the white sheepskin rug at her feet was Birdie! What with excitement, shyness, and fear—yes, fear, for I was terrified lest I said or did something that might betray the emotion within me—my greeting to my lady must have been very incoherent. But she didn't seem to notice anything, and she kissed me and said:

'How nice it is to see you again at last, Emily. You bad girl! Why haven't you been to see us long before this? It was only by chance I saw you coming to-day.'

I stammered something about not wanting to bother her, and she shook her head.

'Nonsense! Of course you wouldn't have bothered me. But never mind, you're here now, and looking so well, too. I was so sorry to hear of the loss of your baby girl. But you're both young—there will be lots of time for others.'

I barely heard what she was saying, for my eyes were fixed upon the child, my baby. There he sat, playing contentedly with a black-faced golliwog doll, and my lady, seeing me staring at him, laughed softly.

'Yes! Here's the baby. Three years old now, and not a baby really any more. Come here, Freddie?' And the child scrambled to his feet and still clutching the golliwog, came

111

obediently to her knee. I could not have spoken then to save my life, but luckily my lady went on talking to him and did not look at me. How beautiful he was! A sturdy, pink-and-white cherub, with a tossing crest of curly brown hair—he had inherited my curly hair—wide blue eyes under arched brows, and a mobile, pretty mouth over a determined little chin. Nothing of Valentine in him that I could see, except perhaps for his pink and white colouring. He was wearing a pale blue velvet suit and a soft white silk blouse, and as he looked up curiously at me I would have given all I had in the world—yes, even my gentle Johnny!—for the right to pick him up in my arms and kiss him until he should struggle to be put down. From far away, as it seemed, I heard myself speak.

'He's lovely, my lady. A lovely boy! You—you must be very proud of him. And happy to have him growing so well.'

My lady smiled again and smoothed his crest of curls with a white ringed hand, and suddenly a wave of savage jealousy swept over me. That hand should have been mine! What right had she—and then I remembered and came to my senses. I didn't have any right any more, I had given it to her—and it was with a dull feeling of inevitability that I heard her reply.

'Yes, I couldn't be happier, or prouder. I'm so glad you came in time to see him before he goes to bed. Now, sonny, I'm afraid it's bath time. Would you ring the bell for nurse, Emily? The bell by the fire-place—pull it three times.'

'Mamma, who's 'at?' It was my boy's voice. He had been staring at me wide-eyed for some minutes, but this was the first time he had spoken.

'That's Emily—Mrs. Bligh,' my lady told him. 'She used to know you when you were a tiny baby. She came to see how well you were growing, and I think she's very pleased with you.'

'Mrs.—Ply,' he pondered gravely. ''at's a funny name. Is she a funny lady?'

My lady laughed.

'I don't think so,' she said merrily. 'She's just a very old friend. Won't you give her a good-night kiss before you go to bed?'

He considered again, then nodded his head, and held up his baby arms to me.

How can I describe my feelings when, for a brief moment, I held my child in my arms again? I know that I was trembling, and when I kissed him it was as though his soft cheek burnt my lips. I dared not hold him for more than a moment, my emotion was rising to such a pitch. And when he put his arms artlessly round my neck and pressed a wet, baby kiss on my cheek in return for mine, it was all I could do to hold myself steady and not burst into tears. I was about to put him down again, when suddenly he twisted round in my arms and made a grab at the shiny-winged beetle among the flowers in my hat. It had only been lightly stitched into place and it came away easily in his hand.

My lady made a shocked exclamation.

'Oh, Freddie, what are you doing? Spoiling Mrs. Bligh's pretty hat like that! How naughty of you!'

She took him out of my arms, he was still firmly clutching the beetle, and scolded him gently, while I—thankful that her attention was concentrated upon him—pulled myself together and adjusted my hat. But to hear my darling scolded was more than I could bear.

'Oh, please, my lady,' I ventured. '*Please* don't be vexed with him? I'm delighted to let him have the beetle. It hasn't spoilt my hat at all.'

Even if it *had*, my heart cried, he could do what he wanted with it, my own, my little one, my darling! Lady Stilwell looked at me doubtfully while Birdie, set down on the rug, examined his new treasure. Mercifully the nurse came in just then and carried him away, and I took my leave, though what I said before I went I can't remember at all clearly. I remember that my lady said she would rescue the beetle when the child was asleep and post it to me, and me telling her most earnestly that I'd like him to keep it. I would, really really! And she looked at me doubtfully and said, Well, she would see,—and so I got away.

*   *   *

Though I thought I had hidden my agitation so well that my lady wouldn't have noticed anything, afterwards I found that she *had*—though she had not, and never did, come anywhere near guessing the real reason for it. She put it down to my sorrow over losing my baby girl being re-awakened by the sight of her child, and she gave me a particularly kind and gentle farewell when I left. I made up my mind not to go again—at any rate not for a long time, not until I was more completely in control of my feelings. The sight of my little son, above all, the warm clinging touch of his baby arms and his soft kiss on my cheek, had shaken me to the core, and for many a night after that meeting I cried myself to sleep, long after Johnny, bless

115

his heart! was snoring happily into the pillow at my side. To see my Birdie, to know that he was safe and well, loved and cared for, was much. But the price in emotional strain was too high for me to pay it very often. So, despite invitations from the Stilwell staff to go and see them whenever the family was in town, I avoided going on one excuse or another. And it was years before I saw my son again.

Miss Beryl was married in the spring of the next year, and what a day it was! More than a day, too. For weeks beforehand everybody was in such a state of excitement that it was no wonder Mrs. Fortescue had a nervous collapse when it was all over, and had to spend several days in bed to recover.

I must say, though, that everything went off wonderfully well. The bride looked lovely in a dress of white brocade and a real Brussels lace veil that cost hundreds of pounds. Miss Sybil and three other young ladies were bridesmaids, in pink moiré silk frocks with wreaths of pink roses in their hair, and bouquets to match. St. Margaret's was so full of flowers that their perfume was too strong for some of the smart ladies, and one or two of them fainted and had to be carried out. It was a great day—and Miss Sybil was in higher spirits than anyone else. For with her sister out of the way, the field was clear for her, and after the wedding was over, she discussed her coming-out party with her mother even more eagerly than before. Mr. Fortescue wasn't very anxious for it, Mrs. Fortescue's maid told me. The wedding had cost him a lot of money and, rich as he was, he was a careful gentleman and kept an eye on his savings. He argued that Miss Sybil was still very young and could well wait another year, which would give him time to recover from the wedding. But Mrs. Fortescue wouldn't have that, and at last Mr. Fortescue shrugged his shoulders and agreed, and a date was fixed. Gunters were engaged to do the catering, an expensive band was booked and the invitations were sent out. And then a blow fell which knocked all parties that season right out—war with the Boers was declared!

England had been a peaceful country for so long that wars had come to seem just a bad sort of dream that happened in the past, and everyone thought that this one couldn't last long. For awhile Mrs. Fortescue went on with her preparations for the big ball. Then one day Mr. Fortescue came home from his office very depressed, and told his wife that the whole idea must be dropped and the party postponed until the war was over. Things, he said, were not going well in South Africa. The Boers were fighting hard and our soldiers didn't seem able to beat them as easily as we had thought they would, and altogether it would be very unwise to give a lavish party when the Government was calling for money to help fight these farmers. To do so, he said, would damage his name and hers, and might possibly affect Miss Sybil's chances in the marriage market. The only thing to do was to cancel all the arrangements. And Miss Sybil had better join one of the ladies' organizations for rolling bandages or knitting socks and so on for the soldiers.

You can imagine the storms and tears when poor Miss Sybil heard the news! But there was nothing to be done but accept the decision, and after awhile she calmed down, and she and her mother plunged into some kind of war work—just what it was, I forget now.

The war dragged on for three years, and before it was over, England had another shock—the Queen died. I suppose it was silly for everyone to feel so surprised, for she was an old lady, eighty-two years of age, and I have no doubt she was glad to go to where her Albert would be waiting for her. But she had been there so long that it was like having the pillars that held up the centre of a house pulled away, and everyone seemed stunned by the news. People all had to go into mourning, and the Park, and the streets, and the shops, looked so queer and sombre. Not a scrap of colour anywhere, not even for children, though children were allowed to wear white, with sashes and hair ribbons of black for the little girls. I put away my own coloured frocks and wore black like the rest, and I was just congratulating myself, when the year of mourning was coming to an end, that soon I could leave off my blacks, when something happened that meant mourning for me in good earnest.

There was a new horse in the stable, one with a tricky temper, and Johnny one day, trying to gentle him into his harness, must have done something to startle or annoy him. He reared up, pawing the air with his front hoofs—and one of them caught Johnny on the head and laid him flat. The other men snatched at the reins and brought the animal down—but it was too late. The flying hoof with its iron shoe had struck my husband on the temple—and he was dead.

Dead! My gentle, kindly Johnny who had loved me so faithfully! And another chapter in my life came to an end.

CHAPTER EIGHT

LIFE MUST GO ON

How TRUE it is that one does not really value a good thing until one has lost it. I'd taken my Johnny as a matter of course, and it wasn't until after his death that I realized how much I loved him, and what fine qualities he had. Night after night, as I lay sleepless upon my bed, I wept in bitter remorse, not only for the loneliness that was now mine, but for the way in which I had treated the dearest and gentlest man any woman had ever had the luck to marry. I had been so absorbed in my trouble about Birdie that I had taken Johnny's love for me for granted, and it had simply never occurred to me to think how much it would have meant to him if I had shown him how dearly I loved him. I *did* love him—loved him very, very much—but I don't believe that I ever once told him so. At any rate, I can never remember doing it, and after he was taken from me it added to my grief that I had been so cruelly remiss.

But however much one suffers, life has to go on, and after the funeral Mrs. Fortescue sent for me, and talked to me very kindly. She and her husband, she said, were very distressed over what had happened. They had liked Johnny so much, and it was tragic that he should have died in such a way. Tragic, too, for me to be left a widow when I was still so young. I must, of course, give up the flat—it would be needed for the new coachman. But would I like to come into the house as head housemaid? I listened dully, and it seemed to me to sound all right. I had to earn my living, and as I was trained to service, I thought this would be as good a way to do it as any other. I knew the routine of the house, and the wages Mrs. Fortescue offered were quite good. Anyway, I had reached a stage by that time where I cared little what happened to me as long as I had food to eat and a roof over my head, and so I accepted the situation.

I sold all the furniture we'd had in the flat—I couldn't bear to be reminded of the happy time when Johnny and I had been together in our little home—and moved into the house in Bryanston Square—and another stage in my life began.

*　　　*　　　*

121

The year of mourning for the old Queen passed away, and the gloomy atmosphere that had engulfed London since her death, passed with it. Colours became bright again, and the round of parties—dinners, luncheons, dances, and At Homes—were resumed. Miss Sybil was at last to have her coming-out party, and her brother, Mr. Arnold, came home from the university for it.

I had only seen him a few times, and I hadn't much liked him. He was a lanky, loose-mouthed, sort of youth, with a drawl and an ultra-showy taste in ties and waistcoats. He was, of course, the apple of his mother's eye, and his sister made a tremendous fuss of him—mainly, I think, because he had a large collection of male friends and might be expected to bring many of them to the house during his vacations. Which meant adding to the number of young men who might be prospective husbands! Miss Sybil was crazy to get married—and, if possible, to marry better than her sister had done.

So home the young gentleman came, and the fuss that was made of him to my mind was simply ridiculous. He brought a titled friend with him, and Miss Sybil and her mother were all smiles, though I thought him a poor little fellow—no taller than I was, with a silly

122

weak face. Still, he was a lord, and that was good enough for the ladies, and certainly he managed to put away enough food and drink to have filled a man twice twice his size.

One night, after dinner, I went upstairs to the bedrooms to turn down the beds and set the brass hot-water cans, swathed in thick towels to keep the water hot, on the wash-stands. I was just finishing the last room when the door opened and in came Mr. Arnold. He stood staring at me a moment, then came towards me. He was between me and the door, unfortunately, and my heart sank, for I'd seen that look in a young man's eyes before—a look that shows he's taken enough drink to make him reckless.

'You're Emily, aren't you?' he said, and his voice was a little blurred. 'Remember seeing you before at my mother's parties. Permanent member of the staff now, eh?'

'My name is Bligh, sir,' I said stiffly. 'I am now house-parlourmaid here. I'd be glad if you would let me pass so that I can attend to my duties.'

He set his back against the door and grinned.

'I'll let you pass when you've paid toll,' he said. 'Come on! Give us a kiss—and then I'll let you go?'

123

'I shall do no such thing!' I said, enraged. 'And now, if you please, sir, get out of my way.'

I came towards him and he made a grab at me. But I sidestepped him, and, before he could touch me, I landed him a real stinger of a slap on the cheek. He was none too steady on his feet from the wine he had drunk at dinner, and he staggered back, away from the door—fortunately he hadn't locked it!—and I was out and off in a flash, panting and furious. I reached my room shaking in mingled rage and humiliation, mixed with uneasiness, too. Still, I hoped that that slap in the face might have taught the young fool to keep his hands off me, and for awhile it did and I was left in peace—that is if one could call it peace with the great coming-out party near at hand and everybody going crazy about it.

For days beforehand, we girls were made to polish silver, and china, and glass, and the reception rooms were all upsidedown with the furniture that had to be cleared away from the big drawing-room for the dancing, and the tables that had to be arranged for the buffet supper in the dining-room. The whole house was in a ferment, and I was thankful when the actual day of the party arrived at last. Early in the morning, Gunter's men came with hampers of food and drinks, and then great armfuls of flowers arrived with a special woman to arrange them from a big flower-shop in the West End. During the afternoon, a bunch of young men came, hired waiters who started to lay the tables, and sort out napkins, spoons, and forks. I was thankful that the waiting was to be done by professional waiters, and not by me and the other girls. We were required to look after the rooms in which the visitors were to leave their wraps, and I was put in charge of the gentlemen's room, Mr. Fortescue's study on the ground floor. I had hopes of making a nice bit of money, as I knew that when the gentlemen were going away they usually left a good tip, especially if they had had plenty to drink. And from the array of bottles I saw displayed, I knew that that night 'plenty' was to be the word!

As I had hoped, I made a really nice little sum of money. Most of the gentlemen left something, and some of the tips were really big. I congratulated myself as I pocketed them, thinking that now I'd be able to restart the nest egg I had once had in the Savings Bank, but which I had spent on buying furniture for Johnny's and my flat. The last gentleman had taken his hat and coat, and I was emptying away the cigar ashes in the ash-trays in the study into the waste-paper basket, when Mr. Arnold walked in. I didn't hear him at first, for the carpet was thick and he walked softly. But a board creaked just behind me, and I whirled round and there he was, grinning at me!

He'd had plenty to drink, that I knew. I had seen him and some of the youngsters sneaking along to the butler's pantry where the drinks were prepared, more than once during the evening, and the butler in charge there had looked at me with raised eyebrows towards the end of the evening, showing what he thought of the liquor they were all consuming. Mr. Arnold had had enough to make him reckless, and before I could escape he'd got me round the waist and was hugging me so tightly that I could hardly breathe.

I'd have smacked him again, but he'd got both my arms pinned down and I could not get them free. I twisted my head that way and this as he tried to kiss me, and struggled desperately to get away. I was panic-striken for fear somebody would come in, for I knew that I'd be blamed if anyone did. It's always the maid's fault in these things, never the master's! As I struggled I thought I heard footsteps outside in the hall and my panic redoubled.

'Oh, Mr. Arnold, let me go! Please let me go?' I panted. 'If anyone comes it will mean the sack for me! Please let me go?'

'Not till I've had that kiss,' he said, grinning like an ape. And slipping one arm round my neck he forced my head forward and kissed me until I was breathless.

Then suddenly he let me go—so suddenly that I almost fell down—as a furious voice rang through the room.

'Arnold! Mrs. Bligh!' said the voice. The worst had happened! Mrs. Fortescue, scarlet with rage, stood in the doorway!

*   *   *

Even now, after all these years, I don't like to remember the awful scene that followed. Mrs. Fortescue lost all her self-control, and screamed at me and her son alternately—but, of course, mainly at me. I was a slut, a common little baggage. I'd been setting my cap at the young master ever since he came into the house. Mr. Arnold tried to defend me, I will say that for him. He swore that it was all his fault and that I had never taken any notice of him—but there was no stemming that torrent of angry words. The upshot of it was that I

127

was sent upstairs to pack my things, and told that I was to clear out of the house first thing in the morning—and without a character!

Though from the moment I had heard her voice I had known that this must happen, my heart sank into my boots when I heard the verdict. Who, in those days, would hire a girl without a reference? I am told that nowadays maids are so hard to get that mistresses will take them without any reference—but it wasn't so then. If you had no written character to show, you could whistle for a job, and I climbed the stairs to my room with an aching heart, feeling bitterly resentful towards all the world, and to Mrs. Fortescue and her son in particular.

I knew that it would be useless to ask for my wages, though we were paid by the month and my money was due to me the very next day. All I had in the world was the few pounds I'd made out of tips from the gentlemen at that fatal party. I packed slowly and drearily, wondering what on earth was to become of me. I didn't bother to undress, but just took off my frock and lay down on the bed, pulling the coverlet over me. I didn't think I would sleep, but I was so tired that I did, and when I woke, it was to see the sun streaming in through the window and a square white envelope lying on the floor near the door, evidently having been pushed under the door while I slept.

I tore it open. It was from Master Arnold.

'I am most terribly sorry,' it said, 'that by playing the fool last night I have landed you in such a mess. I meant no harm really, and I did my best to put things right. I argued with my mother for ages to try to get her to give a reference so that you could get another job, but it was no use, so I suggest you go and see a friend of mine who I know is wanting somebody to look after her little girl. She is a very nice lady who acts on the stage and her name is Miss Cornish. Her address is No 15, Grandison Mews, Cromwell Road. I am sending her a letter about you that should help you to get the place with her, and I hope you will be very happy there. I do want you to understand how very sorry I am for last night.

Yours,
Arnold Fortescue.

P.S. I enclose your wages for the past month, as my mother refuses to pay them herself.'

I drew a long breath of relief. So the silly

young fool had his heart in the right place, after all! I could start afresh, with a little money behind me and the prospect of a new and, I hoped, satisfactory job. I wasn't too anxious to work for a stage lady—I'd always heard that most of them were no better than they should be—and though Master Arnold had mentioned a little girl, he had called her 'Miss,' just as if she wasn't married. But I was in no position to quibble. Here I was, thrown neck and crop out of my place without a character—and here was a job that seemingly didn't need one! I wondered just what Master Arnold had told this Miss Cornish about me and the way in which I had left his mother's employ—but that didn't really concern me; what *did* was that, apparently, she was in need of a maid, and wasn't particular about a reference. I was in luck's way to have a job found for me at all, and the best thing I could do was to go after it as quickly as possible.

I undressed and washed and put on clean clothes, packed my last minute things, and got ready to leave. I left a brief note of farewell on the kitchen table for the cook, saying that there had been a frightful row with Mrs. Fortescue the previous night and she'd sent me off, though it hadn't been my fault at all. Then I picked up my bags and went out of the kitchen into the hall—to find myself face to face with Master Arnold!

Since he never, as a rule, got up till nine o'clock and it was still not seven, I stared at him in astonishment. He looked at me with a sheepish expression and made a dive at my heaviest bag.

'Here, give that to me,' he said gruffly. 'I've been up since dawn, waiting for you. You got my note?'

'Yes, thank you, sir' I said stiffly. Then, for he was still so young, under twenty, I spoke again in a more friendly voice.

'Thank you very much, sir, for giving me the name of your friend, and for saying that you would write to her. I am going to see her to-day.'

'I'm sure she'll take you,' he said as he followed me to the front door, lugging my heavy bag. He reminded me of a dog that had done something it shouldn't, and comes along wagging its tail and looking up into your face to see if it's forgiven. 'I'm sure she'll take you. She's at her wits' end to get somebody, for the kid can't be left. She's only five, but as sharp as a waggon-load of monkeys, and can dance and sing already, fit for any stage. You'll love her!'

'I'm sure I shall, and thank you again, sir,'

131

I said nervously, wishing he wouldn't follow me out on to the steps—early as it was, people might see and wonder. But there was no stopping him! Out he came and hailed a passing cab.

'I'm putting you and your bags into this cab,' he said firmly, 'and I'm paying the cabby. It's the least I can do, so don't start objecting! I'm most awfully sorry I caused you all this trouble. I wouldn't have done it for worlds—but I was tiddley. You know that, don't you? Shake hands and say you forgive me?'

It wasn't possible to go on being angry. The boy was really sorry and was doing his utmost to make amends, I couldn't do anything but shake hands and smile at him and climb into the cab. He gave the address to the driver and paid the fare—and I was off on my new adventure.

CHAPTER NINE

LADY OF THE STAGE

AT FIRST I found the flat at Number Fifteen, Grandison Mews very cramping after the big houses in which I had worked. But I soon got used to it, and since I had to do all the work, except for a woman coming in once a fortnight to do the rough cleaning, I appreciated how much easier it was to live on one level—or rather, two, as the flat was really what is called a 'maisonette.' There were two rooms and a tiny kitchen on the main floor, and two rooms on the floor above. Like the flat I had shared with Johnny, it was over the stables belonging to one of the big houses in the Cromwell Road. But there were no horses in the stable now—the owner of the coach-house was using it for one of the new-fangled motor-cars that were just coming in. Miss Cornish said that motor-cars made a worse smell with their oil and petrol than any horse ever did, but the gentleman who owned the motor-car was a great friend of hers and let her live in the maisonette free, so naturally she couldn't grumble to him, though she used to let off to me now and then.

She was a pretty thing, Miss Cornish, and her little girl was even prettier—black-eyed, with dark curls like bunches of black grapes bobbing on each side of her little round face. I often wondered—though, of course I wouldn't have dreamed of hinting such a thing even to my closest friend—if her papa might not have had a touch of the tarbrush somewhere, since Miss Cornish was as blonde as you like. If her hair wasn't natural yellow, it must have been pretty fair, anyway, for her skin was as white as milk. She was very slim, with a lovely figure, and was a 'show-girl,' as she called it, at a famous theatre called The Gaiety. It meant that she did not dance or sing, but was one of a group of girls chosen just for their looks and their figures. They all had to be the same height, and all they had to do was just to trail about the stage wearing the most wonderful dresses you ever saw. Several times she gave me a ticket for her show, and I never got tired of seeing the glittering scenes, and the dazzling, wonderful, crowds on the stage, though after I'd been back-stage and seen some of them in their dressing rooms, I got more used to them and became what Monsieur called more discriminating.

I got used to going back-stage, too, for Miss Cornish doted on her child to such an extent that she insisted on having her brought round to her dressing-room whenever there was a matinée, to be petted and cooed at by the other actresses and their friends, and by the gentlemen who always seemed to have the run of the ladies' dressing-rooms. I felt quite hot and uncomfortable the first time I went back-stage with little Miss Marianne. We followed a maze of stone corridors until we came to a door marked 'Miss Cornish and Miss Taunton,' and when I had tapped and been told to come in, I nearly fell over backwards with surprise and embarrassment. It was a little room with a screen down one side behind which Miss Taunton was dressing, or undressing and a big mirror fixed to one of the walls with a table before it, littered with pots and jars of powder and paint. There was only one chair and a man was sitting on it with Miss Cornish on his knee—and she only wearing a thin dressing-gown over her drawers and stays!

He was kissing her throat like mad, and she had her eyes closed and her head lolling back in a sort of ecstasy. I must have given a bit of a gasp or something, for she suddenly woke up and sprang off his knee with a giggle, calling out something about 'shocking poor darling Skivvy!'—I had told her my nickname at the Manor one day, and it had tickled her fancy so that she often called me by it instead of Bligh or Emily.

Not that she really minded shocking me. Not she! I don't think anything in the world could have made those stage girls blush or feel ashamed. Miss Taunton came out from behind the screen, wearing precious little more than Miss Cornish, and other folk came in and began fussing round Miss Marianne, and the room got hot and noisy and stank of scent and powder and a lot of other things. I was glad when the interval was over and they all had to go back to the stage, and I was free to take Miss Marianne home.

It wasn't long before I found that Miss Cornish wasn't what's known as a 'good girl.' I suppose it would have been too much to expect her to be, what with her looks and being on the stage and having a baby girl to bring up. I never did discover if she had ever been married, for of course her being called 'Miss' meant nothing at all, all actresses on the stage seemed to be called 'Miss,' whether they were properly wedded or not.

After I'd put the little girl to bed upstairs I wasn't supposed to come down again; but if I left my door open after Miss Marianne had gone to sleep, as I confess I often did as I was frankly curious about the life led by stage girls, I used to hear a lot of what went on below. I used to hear my mistress come back after the show was over, often at one or two in the morning, and nine times out of ten she would come back with some man or other, who didn't leave until nearly dawn. At first I felt rather shocked, but after awhile I got used to it. After all it was none of my business, and it was a comfortable place and well-paid, and Miss Cornish was kind and jolly and very generous with tips and theatre tickets, and gave me all sorts of pretty things when she got tired of them. I might have gone much farther and fared a lot worse.

I soon realized that she was being kept by the gentleman who owned the maisonette and the motor-car. He was a rich City gentleman, with a red face and a thick neck, and very generous he was to her, too. I could see that. Almost every time he came to see her he would bring her something new, an ermine stole and muff, perhaps, or a bit of jewellery, or something pretty to put in her room. The gentleman—Mr. Robinson was his name—was very much in love with her, and she used to pet him and call him darling and all sorts of fancy names, though I very soon knew she wasn't a bit in love with him, any more than she was with any of the other gentlemen she used to come home with. She was in love with the fellow who had been in her dressing-room the first time I went there, the one who had had her on his knee. He was called Mario, and he played the leading fiddle in the orchestra of the theatre where she acted; and it was he who came home with her most often and stayed with her all night usually until I served breakfast to her about ten o'clock in the morning.

She made no bones about him to me, and I marvel sometimes now how soon one can get used to a person living that way—though what my grandmother would have said to me carrying in breakfast to a lady and gentleman in bed together who weren't married to each other, I don't like to think!

Miss Gertie, as I used to call her, used to tease me sometimes when I went in, and would say things like 'We must shock our darling Skivvy, Mario!' And sometimes he'd laugh and say something teasing, too, but mostly he was silent and moody and would only grunt. He was a handsome chap, with a fine, tall figure, and a head covered with silky black curls. At first I thought that maybe he was little Marianne's father, but, later, I found that he couldn't be, for Miss Cornish only met him a few months before I went to her, when she went to act in the theatre where he was fiddling.

He was a fine fiddler. Sometimes he'd bring his fiddle along with him when he came back with her after the show was over, and play to her. I used to set my door wide open then and lie and listen, and I could understand how he felt when he used to rage sometimes and declare that he'd die if he had to spend all his life playing in a damned theatre orchestra. He ought to be playing at big concerts, he said, with thousands of people listening, and Miss Gertie would pet him and cosset him and tell him that she *knew* he would one day make good and be known for the great musician that he was. And after a bit he would quiet down and eat his supper, and they would be happy again.

Yet, somehow, I always felt sorry for her. I think I knew by a sort of instinct that she loved him much more than he loved her. I soon became sure that all he really wanted of her was an attractive body to sleep with, and a nice, convenient flat to go to for food and petting and drink. But she was quite sure that he was passionately in love with her, and was forever talking about how, when his luck turned, they'd get married. She even turned down two gentlemen who wanted to marry her, because she was so crazy about Mr. Mario and so certain that one day she would be married to him.

Her friend, Miss Taunton, who shared her dressing-room at the theatre used to scold her for losing her chances.

'Mario's just making use of you until something better comes along,' was what Miss Taunton said in my hearing one day—and didn't I agree with her! But Miss Gertie was so angry that she wouldn't speak to her for several days, and after that Miss Taunton just shrugged her shoulders and said no more.

Yes! It was an ill-fated love that poor young lady had for her Mario—ill-fated is the word, as you'll see a little later on. It was a strange chapter in my life that I spent with her, and looking back now it seems like a sort of dream. But there was one real thing that came out of the dream—and that was my meeting with my darling Monsieur.

* * *

It is odd to think that they say now that the name of Jacques Yvetôt is famous. When I
140

knew him he was very far from famous. He was poor and not even young, a dreamer and an idealist who had spent his life in pursuing his dreams and had been happy doing it, though it had brought him little in the way of luck or money. But I must begin at the beginning to tell you about him.

Mr. Arnold had been right when he had said that Miss Marianne was as sharp as a waggon-load of monkeys. She was only five years old, but she could lisp out a song in time and tune, and dance, too, in a marvellous way for a moppet of that age. And was Miss Cornish proud of her! She got round Mr. Robinson to pay for special dancing lessons for her, and when there was a special *Café Chantant* Show put on by some Society lady for charity, she somehow managed to get Marianne tried out for it, and when it was held, Marianne carried off the prize. She did what was called a 'coon' dance and song, and when she skipped on to the stage and started singing 'O Honey, ma Honey,' as clear and confident as if she was her mama's age, you could have heard a pin drop in the theatre, and afterwards, when she'd done her little dance, how the audience clapped her!

Miss Cornish was half daft with pride, and nothing would content her but to have the child's picture painted, in that coon costume, if you please! Mr. Robinson said she could have it done if it wasn't too dear, but he wasn't going to pay a Royal Academician's fee for a mere baby. It was Mr. Mario who suggested Jacques Yvetôt. He'd done one or two poster designs for the show in which Miss Cornish was playing. He was a good artist, but not famous, so he'd be cheap. Mario knew him a little, and he undertook to ask him to come along to discuss the matter. So it happened that one evening when Miss Cornish was at the theatre and I had just given Miss Marianne her supper and was about to put her to bed, there came a ring at the doorbell, and I went down to answer it.

I guessed who it was the minute I saw him, for I had heard Mario describing him. A small man with some trouble in the spine that gave the effect of a hump. He was wearing a shabby brown velvet coat and a French *béret* pulled forward over his eyes, and he was carrying an armful of things—a flat colour box, a folding easel, two or three canvases strapped together and a campstool. His clean-shaven face was very thin, and a shock of prematurely white hair poked out from under his *béret*.

'Mees Cornish?' he asked. His accent was

pretty, although he had lived and worked in London for many years, he had never lost his accent. When I said that she had just gone to the theatre, he grimaced like a disgusted child.

'*Tiens*! But wait!' He looked at me eagerly. 'Perhaps you know, Mees, why I come here?'

'I think I do,' I said cautiously. 'Aren't you the Musseer Eeveto who's going to paint Miss Cornish's little girl?'

'*Mais oui!* Yes, yes. So she is the one I should see. Is it possible to see her, Mees?'

'Yes, she hasn't gone to bed yet,' I said, standing back for him to come in. 'If you'll come up to the drawing-room, sir, I'll bring her to you.'

As he climbed the steep little flight of stairs leading to the maisonette I heard him mutter, half to himself:

'Mother's darling—yes, yes! All mothers' darlings are lovely to them, but not at all lovely to me. If she is just another stupid, bun faced *enfant*—'

'Oh, but she isn't,' I interrupted indignantly. 'She's as pretty as a picture and *clever!* You should just see her dance!'

He followed me into the pretty cluttered-up living-room, with its fluffy satin cushions and myriad china ornaments, and all the rest of

143

the fripperies that Miss Cornish loved to have around her, and, for a moment, he stood still and stared about him with an odd expression on his face. Then he turned briskly to me.

'Yes, I have heard of her dancing, but it is to paint that I am commissioned. Can I see the child? No, don't fetch her—let me come and see her where she is.'

He had a gift with children, had Monsieur. Sleepy and a little fretful as Miss Marianne was, she yielded to him at once. He showed her how to make a shadow-rabbit with his twisted fingers on the wall behind her bed, and when he taught her the old game of 'Here's the Church and here's the Steeple,' she shouted with delight and could only with difficulty be prevailed upon to let him go. Closing the door of her room behind him at last, he picked up his gear.

'A charming child! Why must her silly mother insist that she is painted in that stupid dress? I would rather paint her as I have just seen her, in her nightdress, playing with sha-dows on the wall and with all the world of dreams and fancies in her eyes. Well, tell Mees Cornish I will do as she wishes.'

He descended a few steps of the stairs and then turned to look up at me.

'You can bring the child—and that foolish

costume—to my studio? To-morrow at eleven o'clock for the preliminary studies. Number 22, Museum Buildings Bloomsbury. It is at the top of a tall old house, so you will have to climb many stairs, but at the top is air and peace and quiet. *Au revoir*!'

He ran down the rest of the flight, there was the sound of a slammed door, and he was gone.

* * *

Monsieur Yvetôt's studio was, as he had said, at the top of a tall, gloomy old building in Bloomsbury, facing the British Museum, and Miss Marianne and I were both panting by the time we had climbed the seemingly-interminable flight of uncarpeted stairs. The little landing on which we stood waiting was dingy and dark, but when the door was opened and we walked into the painter's studio, the gloom vanished. Evidently two attics had been knocked together to make one large room, and since half the roof was glass, this made the place bright and cheerful at once.

There was plenty of colour in it. The walls were lined with pictures, some finished, some only rough sketches. There was an ancient, but brightly patterned carpet spread on the bare boards, though it was so covered with dust and fluff that my house-trained fingers itched for a dustpan and brush. A curtain of red Turkey twill hung part-way across the far end of the room, behind which showed one end of a divan bed on which lay a fat brown and white spaniel. I was to find later that the curtain also hid a battered cooking stove, and an old dresser littered with crockery and pots and pans and heaven knows what else beside! In one corner of the room there stood a Victorian screen covered with stuck-on coloured pictures and valentines. Behind this screen, Monsieur's models dressed and undressed. The rest of the furniture consisted of a painted Italian chest which housed Monsieur's clothes, a chair or two, and a scored and smeared old table on which reposed several jars full of brushes, a spare palette, some socks and ties, a plate with bread and cheese on it, and a dirty cup that had contained coffee. And, of course, reigning supreme over all, a tall easel, on which was a canvas representing, so Monsieur told me later, Diana reposing after the chase.

I stopped, shocked and frowning. This was certainly not the sort of thing I thought it right for a child as young as Miss Marianne to see. Monsieur, following my gaze, began to laugh. The spaniel, hearing the sound, lumbered off the bed and came towards us wagging its tail. Its name, I found, was Towser, and I was relieved to see that it was friendly. While Miss Marianne was petting the creature, Monsieur took the picture off the easel, propping it up in a distant corner; then he put a fresh canvas on the easel and spoke to the model who was dressing behind the screen.

'Ready to go, Clara? My next sitter's here.'

The model, a pert little piece, dressed in a common sort of way, came from behind the screen. She gave me a cheeky nod as I stood red-cheeked with disapproval—I was a real prig in those days, but, thanks to Monsieur I learnt better after a time—and went to look critically at her picture.

'S'not bad,' she said. 'Though I think I got better thighs than those what you've give me. Want me again?'

'Yes, come again to-morrow,' Monsieur told her. 'And don't try to criticise something you know nothing about. Your body's a good one as bodies go, but I've made it better than God did.'

'You're a card, you are!' the girl said, turning towards the door. 'All right, I'll be here. Tootle-oo, and if you can't be good, be careful!'

The door slammed behind her, and Monsieur cocked an amused eyebrow at me.

'She's a character, that one, *n'est-ce pas*, Madame? What we call in France *une drôle*.'

'She's got no manners,' I said severely. 'She never even called you sir.'

He gave a snort of laughter.

'Nor she did! But don't forget that this is Bohemia, not Mayfair, not even Pimlico or Belgravia!' He squatted down suddenly on his heels before Miss Marianne who was watching him fascinatedly, and making a frightful grimace produced a burst of laughter from the child. As before, in a matter of minutes she was eating out of his hand, as the saying is, and she made no demur when I took her behind the screen and dressed her in the striped trousers, white blouse, and floppy straw hat of the coon character she was supposed to portray. While I was undressing her, Monsieur had dragged a little stool to a position from which he could watch us, and was busily sketching her. I was frowning again with disapproval when I found what he was doing, for I don't hold with a man looking on while a little girl is undressed. I didn't realize then what I later came to know—that when Monsieur was in pursuit of the art he loved it was waste of time trying to stop him.

He was a lightning worker, at least in the early stages of a picture, and he needed to be for Miss Marianne. She had no notion of standing still for more than a brief moment or two, and bounced here and there like a piece of quicksilver, playing with Towser, climbing on the furniture, running all over the place and asking questions nineteen to the dozen. Monsieur would laugh and tease her and answer her questions, and all the time be sketching, sketching—making dozens of little rough pictures of her, throwing down one sheet as fast as it was covered and seizing another until the floor all round him was littered with sheets of paper like leaves in autumn.

I watched him fascinated, wondering why he didn't order the child to stand still so that he could make a proper drawing of her. But that wasn't Monsieur's way. He would make a whole series of lightning sketches, and from them build up his picture, and it was this method I was told long afterwards, that resulted in the vivid lifelike portraits he made, as contrasted with the carefully-posed photographic pictures made by most artists of his day.

The first time he did not keep us more than about half an hour. At the end he gave Miss

Marianne a glass of milk and a piece of cake, and as I washed up glass and plate at the little sink behind the red curtain, my heart really ached for the poor little man who lived in such a clutter of dirt and disorder. I wondered if he would be offended if the next time we came I did a bit of tidying up while he painted, and I resolved to ask him. I didn't think he would mind—he was so kind and friendly, and I did appreciate his calling me 'Madame' as though I was a lady, instead of just using my surname as most people did.

When we left, Miss Marianne put up her face to him to be kissed, and he picked her up in his arms and held her for a moment before putting her down.

'*Au'voir, ma petite mignonne,*' he said tenderly. 'Be a good girl to your *maman* and to the kind little Madame here, and come again to-morrow for me to make a pretty picture of you.'

As he put her down he held out his hand to me. I held out mine, a trifle surprised, for it was not the habit of gentlemen to shake hands with servants. I was more surprised still when he bent and kissed the back of it.

'*Au Revoir*, Madame,' he said, 'And my thanks to you for bringing *la petite* to me.'

As I went down the steps, there was no

denying that I felt sort of pleased at what he had done. Just for a minute I hadn't been Skivvy at all—I'd been a woman who was used to being treated respectfully by real gentlemen. For I was sure that Monsieur Yvetôt, though he might be a poor out-at-elbows artist on the surface, was a real gentleman, and somehow it gave me a good feeling.

* * *

After that first morning, I lost all my shyness of Monsieur, and when we next went along to the studio I ventured to take with me a brush and duster. When I asked him if, while he got on with his painting, I might be allowed to do a little bit of dusting and tidying rather than have to sit idle, he raised surprised eyebrows, but said with obvious pleasure that it was *gentille* of me to suggest such a thing, and if I really wished—

I *did* wish, for I was never a one to sit twiddling my thumbs. And after that I spent every moment I was there in trying to clean up the place—and was it a job! He had never been able to afford to pay a woman to do any cleaning, and though one or two of his models—that girl Clara, for instance—sometimes offered to try to get the place into some sort of order, they simply didn't seem to know what cleaning was. All they ever did, as far as I could see, was to sweep the dust under the divan and the stove, and hide the dirty plates and pans inside the cupboard.

It took me days of hard work to get things anything like shipshape. But at last the room really began to look something like a gentleman artist's home should look. The curtains fairly shrieked to be washed, but I hadn't the time to tackle them, with only an hour, at most, to cram everything into. But I could tell that Monsieur was pleased at what I did do by the way he looked round the room and then, with a nod of satisfaction, returned to his painting. On the last day, when the picture was finished, he produced a box of sweets for Miss Marianne, and for me, a bottle of French perfume tied up with a big bow of pink satin ribbon. I had never been given anything so luxurious before, and a lump seemed to come into my throat as he bowed in that little ceremonious way he had and handed the bottle to me.

For a few moments I was tongue-tied, while I turned it about and about in my hands—almost, he told me long afterwards, as though I was a 'Roman' and the bottle a holy relic. But he seemed satisfied at my reaction and gave his quick little nod.

'I see you like my little gift. I am glad. I want to say *merci* for your so-great kindness, Madame, in putting my poor house in order. Now I see it looking as it should I am covered with gratitude, and so glad I have found something that pleases you.'

'Oh, indeed,' I stammered. 'It's the prettiest thing I ever saw. Though when I can use it, Monsieur, I cannot think.'

He raised his eyebrows whimsically.

'But why? Surely you have your time off from looking after this little one? Wear a drop when you go out with your *amant*, and he will be at your feet. Is it not named "Nuit d'Amour"?'

I knew what 'Amour' meant, and I shook my head.

'I haven't a young man,' I said. 'I'm a widow and have to work for my living. I'm not a fine lady, you know, only a skivvy!'

'Skivvy? That is a funny little word. It means a servant—one who serves? Well, but service is honourable, Madame, and you serve well, that I know. Otherwise this little one would not be so fond of you and so obedient.'

'Oh, I suppose I'm a good servant, as far as that goes,' I said.

It was odd, but at the time it never struck

me how curious it was that I could talk so frankly and easily to a gentleman like Monsieur. I think it was because he was so unselfconscious—I think that is the word—himself. Just one human being talking to another, so that, for the moment, position and class and all that faded into the background. Nonsense they are really, I know, for the good God made us all the same flesh and blood, and nowadays there's not half so much stress laid upon class-distinctions as in the same time of which I am talking. But it was strange that I should have been able to speak so naturally to Monsieur then.

He looked at me attentively, as I settled Miss Marianne's frilled white muslin hat on her dark curls. Then he said:

'If you are tired of being a skivvee, you could always earn a living by being a model, you know?'

I stared at him, thinking he was joking, but he went on:

'I am not teasing you, Madame. I am serious. I am an artist and I have watched you, and I know that you are most excellently well-proportioned, and models with really good figures are not easy to find.'

'But,' I said incredulously, 'I'm not pretty.'

Monsieur laughed.

'No, you are not strictly pretty, it is true, though you have a piquant little face—a face one likes to see come round the door. But you have a *very* pretty body—and the body is what an artist looks at first.'

'You mean you'd want to draw me without any clothes on?' I asked indignantly. 'Oh, I never—'

He raised a hand to silence me.

'I do not insult you, Madame. I assure you that I, who am old enough to be your father, even perhaps your grand-father, do not make this suggestion with any thought of danger to that virtue which you British hold so dear.'

I flushed and bit my lip, feeling foolish, and he went on, more gently:

'To an artist, a model is a lay figure— especially to an old artist such as I am, who has looked on many lovely women, clothed and unclothed. I like and respect my models, and pay them as well as I can afford to do when they sit for me. But to me they are just living dummies—that is all.'

I broke into an embarrassed laugh.

'I'm sorry, Monsieur. It's impossible for me, but I see what you mean, and I'm sorry I—I'm sorry—'

I halted, unable to find the words I wanted, and he finished the sentence for me.

155

'Sorry you jumped to unjustified conclusions? That is all right, Madame Sk—no, I will not use that name. Your first name, please? Emily? Ha, that is better. Madame Emilie. So now we understand each other Madame Emilie, and you are not cross with Monsieur any more, eh? I make the suggestion, but it does not please you, so we will forget it and still be friends?'

'Yes, indeed,' I said eagerly. 'I'm sorry I was so stupid. And I'm sorry, too, I haven't been able to put this place really to rights, sir. If only there had been a few more sittings, I could have made it look so much better.'

'Well,' said Monsieur, 'if Madame Emilie likes to pay her friend Monsieur a visit now and then when she has the time off, and can do a little cleaning when she comes, he will be very grateful. Only he will pay her for her work, because that is right and proper—no, no arguing! Besides, since we are friends, I should like to know sometimes how things go with you, my child.'

His eyes looked kindly into mine.

'Also, I would like to know how things go with *la mère* of the little one here. *Hélas*, these fair, frail women! Their beauty is so often a will-o'-the-wisp, leading them into a dismal swamp at last.'

Miss Cornish had come with us twice to see how the portrait was getting on, looking her loveliest and bringing with her so much perfume that it had scented the studio long after she had gone. The first time she had come with Mr. Robinson, the second, with her lover, Mario. It was plain that the situation had been summed up by this shrewd little Frenchman. There was nothing I could say in reply to his words, especially with the child there, but as I turned to leave he said in a low voice which Miss Marianne, busy with the dog, could not hear:

'Madame Emilie, I sense tragedy there. I am of Brittany where we are what you would call "fey", and it is rare for me to be mistaken. If trouble comes, do not forget that in Jacques Yvetôt you have a friend upon whom you can call for help at any time. At any time!'

As I went down the long flight of stairs, I had a warm feeling in my heart. I felt that Monsieur had spoken the truth. He was my friend—and time was to prove him so. The best friend I ever had.

CHAPTER TEN

A CHANCE ENCOUNTER

MISS CORNISH was enchanted with the finished painting of her little girl, and, indeed, it was a pretty thing. A dark blue night sky, with a big yellow moon showing behind a group of black trees, and the little figure dancing in a moonlit patch, bright in its red and white striped trousers, white blouse, and great straw hat. But in the end it was the picture that brought about the tragedy which Monsieur, with that queer second-sight that I was to grow to know so well, had foreseen.

So pleased was Miss Cornish with the picture that she gave a special party at a big hotel to show it off, and she invited, among other people, the Society lady who had let Miss Marianne dance at her *Café Chantant*. An American lady she was, very wealthy, who had married an English lord and was now a widow of about fifty—Lady Enderby. I think, maybe, if she had been an English lady she wouldn't have come to a party given by a show girl—for ladies and show girls didn't mix then as they do now. But being American, she was different, and Miss Cornish was very triumphant when she said she'd come. It was to be a big party and Miss Marianne was to dance again. After everybody had seen the picture there was to be a sort of variety show. Miss Cornish knew lots of stage folk and there was no difficulty in getting people to come and do their acts—and this, Miss Cornish told Mario, was his big chance. He would be one of the star turns with his fiddle, and, who knew, this American lady, who was so rich, might be the one to give him the opportunity to escape from being a mere orchestral player and become a concert violinist.

I forget now the name of the hotel in which the party was given, but it was a big place, and the party was held in a large room with a stage built across one end. There were drinks served while people circulated round the picture and asked who was the painter— Monsieur had been invited but he wouldn't come—and afterwards the easel with the picture on it was put on one side, and the guests sat at little tables eating all kinds of good things and drinking champagne, while the curtain went up on the stage and the show began.

How Miss Cornish and Mr. Mario managed to get out of their regular engagements at the theatre I never knew, but manage it they did. Miss Cornish looked lovely—the American lady looked nothing beside her, though she was loaded with diamonds—in her hair, and round her neck, and diamond bracelets all up her arms. She was a lean, restless-looking little woman, with a hard mouth and a pair of dark eyes that were forever roving over the people and things around her. Maybe she might have been attractive in her youth, but I think she'd always have been the greedy type, snatching at what she wanted, no matter to whom it belonged—and she ran true to type all right, as things turned out.

There was a juggler who gave a turn, and somebody who played the zither, and a pretty girl who sang, but no other dancing than Marianne's, for Miss Cornish was determined she should have no rival. For the same reason Mario was the only musician. As he came forward with his violin under his arm and bowed to the audience, I realized afresh how handsome he was, and I wondered if it would be his fiddling or his appearance that would appeal most to Lady Enderby. I peeped from the side of the stage where I was waiting on Miss Marianne, who was due to go on when Mr. Mario had played his piece, and I saw that she had her eyes fixed on him, and at the end she was one of the most enthusiastic in her applause. Certainly he played wonderfully, and he had to play again, they were shouting 'Encore! Encore!' so hard.

Yes! He made a hit all right. He and the child were the star turns of the evening, and Miss Cornish was wild with delight and excitement when I helped her to get to bed that night. I hoped that his success was going to result in happiness for her, for though she wasn't a good girl—and there were times when my conscience worried me about working for her when she led such a shameless sort of life—I couldn't help but be fond of her. She was so sweet and kind, and so generous. She would give the clothes off her back to anybody she was sorry for, and she lent money to anybody who asked for it—from beggars in the street to her own stage friends.

'Money burns a hole in my pocket, Skivvy,' she would say—and she was right. I tried to stop her wasting it, and did my best to get her to put a little by each week in the Savings Bank, but she wouldn't listen to me and at last I gave up trying. She wasn't made to be saving and careful; she was just a heedless, sweet-natured baby, and, for all the naughty way she lived, I couldn't help but love her, and I worried over what would happen to her when she grew older and lost her looks and didn't attract men any more. But there! As things turned out I didn't need to worry about that, and perhaps what happened was the best thing for her, after all, terrible as it was at the time.

*　　　　*　　　　*

A few days after the party, when I had put Miss Marianne to bed, I found that Miss Cornish had left her bag behind. I knew she'd need it at the theatre, so I thought I had better go down and leave it with the stage door-keeper. There was a decent woman next door who used to come in now and then when a bit of extra help was needed, so I called her in to keep an eye on the child and went out on my errand. I had left the bag, and was walking down the Strand to catch a bus back home, when I passed a girl strolling along with the apparently aimless but really purposeful walk of the street-walker. I was used to seeing this sort of girl by now, and I seldom glanced at them as I went by. But there was something about the loitering figure of this girl that stirred my memory. I paused and looked back at her and found that she was looking back, too. Then she came towards me and stood staring at me—and of all the people in the world, it was Tilda!

Tilda! Tilda a street-walker! I was so shocked that for a moment I could not speak. Yet, in a way, I wasn't really astonished. I can see now that, from the beginning, Tilda had been heading for that sort of life, with her readiness to kiss and cuddle with any man who fancied her. But remembering her as my bright-eyed, merry little friend of my early days at the Manor, I found it difficult to accept.

'Well! If it isn't Skivvy!' Her eyes, less bright than of old and ringed with lashes weighted with mascara, took me in from head to foot. 'Fancy meeting you! Well, well! Aren't you going to say you're glad to see me?'

I swallowed hard. Glad? Yes, in a sense I was glad—but in this way—

'Tilda! What a surprise,' I managed at last. 'I've always wondered what happened to you after you left the Manor. Mrs. Dibben told me you'd gone, but she didn't know where you were, and you never answered the letters I wrote to you.'

She laughed and threw back her head, and I saw in the light from a chemist's shop by which we were standing, how thickly her face was smeared with paint and powder. She was dressed in a showy sort of dress, with dangling gilt ear rings in her ears and a lot of bangles on her wrists, and she was reeking with some strong kind of scent, while her eyes glanced from side to side as she talked to me, keeping a sharp look-out for a likely man.

'Well, now you can see what happened,' she said in her old impudent way. 'I went off with Jimmy Levett—you remember him, don't you? One of the grooms at the Manor.'

'Jimmy Levett? But—' I began.

Tilda interrupted me.

'Yes, he was married. But of course he got the sack, and after a bit we got sick to death of each other. He went back to his wife, and though the Stilwells wouldn't have him back they got him a place somewhere or other and for all I know he's in it still. As for me, I tried various jobs, but I find men an easier way of earning a living than anything else—and here I am!'

I did not know what to say to this barefaced avowal of the way she lived, and she grinned at me mischievously.

'Still the same prim old Skivvy! But, of course, you're a respectable woman now, aren't you? Married young Bligh, didn't you? I suppose you've got a whole row of brats by this time?'

I found my voice at last.

'I'm a widow,' I said. 'Johnny died two years ago—got kicked on the head by a horse in the stable. We only had one child, a little girl who died as a baby.'

Tilda's grin faded.

'Oh, I'm sorry. I didn't know. After Jimmy and I parted company I didn't hear no more news from the Manor. Come and have a drink and a talk Skivvy?'

Then, as I shook my head, she said in a rather bitter tone:

'I suppose you're too high and mighty to be seen drinking with a girl like me. Though, come to think of it, except that you were lucky enough to get married and I wasn't, there's not much to choose between us that I can see! What about your Birdie? *He* wasn't got in a respectable marriage-bed, exactly, was he!'

The taunt aroused me and I rounded on her fiercely.

'You shut up about him!' I snapped. 'That's all past and done with and forgotten now.'

'Forgotten?' said Tilda. 'You've not forgotten! If you had, you wouldn't be bristling up the way you're doing now! I see bits about him in the papers—"Lord and Lady Stilwell and their handsome little son." "The Honourable

Freddie Stilwell, page at his sister's wedding!" Lord! How I laugh when I see things like that and remember who the kid really is!'

By this time I was livid with anger.

'If you say another word about him, Tilda, I'll hit you in the face so that you'll have to try to get your next man with a broken nose!' I said, and Tilda backed against the chemist's window and put up a protesting hand.

'Hey, stop! I'm sorry, Skiv! Don't take on so, I was only funning. I won't say another word, I promise. I must go now, but tell me where you're working and let's meet on your afternoons off. We was good friends in the old days, and I haven't got too many friends now.'

The wistful note in her voice touched me, and I remembered how she had, indeed, proved herself a loyal friend. I hesitated, but wariness prevailed and when I spoke it was to refuse her request, though I worded my refusal as kindly as I could.

'I'm working for a lady and a little girl and I don't get much time off. I'm sorry, Tilda, I suppose you'll say I'm sticking my nose in the air—but, well, I've been a decent-living girl since that one slip-up, and I loved my Johnny, and I'd feel I was letting him down if I kept company with anyone leading your sort of life. I'm sorry—'

But Tilda had already turned away.

'Oh, that's all right,' she said, with a bitter edge to her voice. 'You always were a prig, Skivvy, and you ain't altered, not a mite, so I guess I'm not losing much!'

She minced off in her high-heeled shoes, and with a queer feeling of pain in my heart I went on my way. Poor Tilda! To see her as she was now, lined and prematurely aged by the vile life she was leading, and to remember the pretty little maid at the Manor House who had been my friend, hurt and saddened me. I told myself that, since, it appeared the Strand was her 'beat,' I would try and avoid going there in the evening hours, which were, I knew, the usual time for street-walkers to go abroad.

So I found Tilda—and lost her in the shadows from which for that brief meeting she had emerged. But I was to see her again—and in circumstances that even now send a shudder through me to remember.

*   *   *

I forget just when it was that I first realized that things were not going well between Miss Cornish and her lover, Mario. The American

167

lady, Lady Enderby, had taken a great fancy to Mr. Mario, and very soon after she met him at Miss Cornish's party, she asked him to play for her at one of her musical evenings. Miss Cornish was asked, too, that first time, and she was delighted when Mr. Mario was again a great success. She brought him back to her flat when it was over, and they drank to the wonderful future they would share together now that he was really on the way to fame. But when Lady Enderby gave a second party and asked Mr. Mario and *not* Miss Cornish, Miss Cornish was terribly upset. And when it happened a *third* time, there was a regular royal row!

It was in vain that Mr. Mario tried to soothe her. She wanted him to promise that he wouldn't play for a musical evening again unless she was invited, and when he refused to promise, they had a furious quarrel. My! How they went on at one another! As I bathed Miss Marianne and put her to bed, I could hear the shouting and the swearing as plainly as though I had been in the room with them. When at last Mario flung out of the flat in a rage, and I went to my pretty, foolish, over-loving Miss Gertie, I found her drowned in tears, lying across the pink satin sofa. It was eight o'clock and she should already have been at the theatre, dressed and ready to lead the line of beautiful girls on to the stage, but she was so demented with jealous misery that I had quite a difficulty in making her look at the clock, and when at last she did, her face was so ravaged and drawn that my own eyes filled with tears, too. It was plain that she couldn't possibly appear on the stage, so she scribbled a note to the manager and told me to get a cab and take it to the theatre. I did as she had asked, but in her misery she forgot that she had promised to have supper with Mr. Robinson after the show, and when he didn't see her on the stage as usual—he had a special stall and paid for it every night whether he was able to go or not—he came round to see what was the matter. She got into a panic when she heard his voice at the door, and tore off her clothes and scuttled into bed, and sent me to give him a drink and explain that she had a severe stomach attack. And then Mr. Robinson panicked, too, and sent for her doctor, and when he came Miss Gertie had to pretend like mad that she had been sick and faint, and I had to back her up and lie as hard as ever I could to him. Dear me, that was an evening and a half! And when at last the doctor and Mr. Robinson had departed, lo and behold, in came Mr. Mario, bursting with excitement and saying that he had met an American impresario—Monsieur told me that was the proper name for a gentleman who specialized in launching musical geniuses—and had so impressed him that he was to play for him at a private party he was giving in his hotel the next week. So Miss Cornish and her Mario fell into each other's arms and made it up, and the evening ended, as so many evenings did, with me frying bacon and eggs and making coffee for them at two o'clock in the morning, and them talking and making love until dawn!

That was an odd time I lived through then, with odd happenings and odd people, and only Monsieur to keep me in mind that there were sane and sensible people in the world as well. I used to visit Monsieur occasionally, not too often in case I wore out my welcome, but he always seemed pleased to see me and I *did* enjoy the times I went there. I went often enough to keep the studio more or less decent, and when I had done my work, I would make tea and we would sit down and drink it together and talk—and the more I knew of that little man, the more interesting I found him.

He was the son of poor fisher-folk in Brittany, and as far back as he could remember he used to go out fishing with his father. But he'd always had an itch to paint, and when he could he made sketches with colours and canvas given to him by an artist who came to lodge in his father's house. When he was about fifteen, his father was drowned one night in a storm, and his mother died soon afterwards from shock and a broken heart. Then he left the village and tramped to Paris and went to the studio of the artist who had given him the paints, and the artist took the poor lad in and fed him and got clothes for him, and from that moment he became determined to earn his living as an artist. It took a long time before he was able to, of course, but he did all kinds of odd jobs by day, and at night went to art classes, and somehow he managed to exist and learnt how to paint as well.

Later he fell in love with the daughter of a farmer whom he met in a village outside Paris where he had gone to help with the harvest. They had married and for a little while had been very happy. But she had died in childbirth and the child had died, too, and after that Monsieur gave up any thought of marrying again. And then, later still, he had come to England and had settled down in London, where he made enough by his painting to live in tolerable comfort though he never in his lifetime became famous or rich.

They were pleasant meetings and I enjoyed them to the full. It was the first time in my life that I had been able to talk to someone who was intelligent and well-read, for Monsieur, although he had been given very little schooling, had read and studied every book he could lay his hands on, and he had a wonderful memory, so that his mind was stocked with information upon all manner of subjects. He had talked, too, with many men of culture and breeding, and, as I was to learn, could converse with them with knowledge and wisdom on equal terms.

So life went on—then suddenly a bombshell fell upon my poor, pretty mistress. The American impresario wanted Mr. Mario to throw up his job with the theatre orchestra and go out to America to give a series of concerts—and without a moment's hesitation, Mario accepted his offer. He sent in his resignation from the orchestra and then came rushing round to the flat to tell Miss Cornish. I had been out with Miss Marianne for a walk, and when we came in they were hard at it—him storming and she crying her eyes out. She wanted to chuck her job at the theatre and go with him, and he was shouting at her that he didn't want her. He wouldn't have her trailing round with him as though he were a Victorian girl and she his chaperone. It was too absurd!

'Here have I got my big chance at last, and you want to spoil it! Don't be a fool, Gertie! Can't you see that it's far better for me to go out with no strings attached and nothing to divert my mind? When I've made the hit I'm certain I can make—then you can come over if you like.'

'I wouldn't be in your way,' she wept. 'I'd stay in the background until you wanted me.'

'How *could* you stay in the background? You're too pretty, and the papers would be all over the story of your leaving the theatre to come with me. We aren't married—what sort of publicity do you think it would be for me? The very worst!'

'We could get married before we went,' she said.

I saw his eyes flicker as he glanced at her sideways. I couldn't help seeing, for the drawing-room door was wide open and I had to pass it to get the little girl upstairs, and I knew that my suspicions had been right all along. He had no intention of marrying her. She was just a pretty plaything, and now he wanted no more of her. If he ever married anyone, it would be somebody who could help him in his ambition, not a sweet, foolish, penniless piece of womanhood like Gertie Cornish.

'I've told you often enough that I don't intend to marry until I can keep a wife in style,' he told her. 'I'm going to storm this citadel alone—then we'll see.'

'Are you so sure you're going alone?' she asked acidly. 'Are you sure Lady Enderby won't be on the same boat?' And then they went off again in the old way, until at last he flung himself out of the flat in a rage, and she cried herself into an exhausted sleep. How often had I witnessed this scene! But this time it was more serious.

Less than a week later, I read in the paper that Lady Enderby was planning to go to New York where her protégé Signor Mario Buanalozzi, the young violinist who had aroused so much interest at her recent parties, was to be launched on a series of concerts organized by the well-known impresario Mr. Abram Solomons, and my heart sank. So it was true! Lady Enderby was going with him, and I felt certain that she was either Mario's mistress already, or had every intention of becoming so. I would have given a lot to have been able to avoid taking the paper to Miss Cornish, but she would only have demanded to know where it was if I had not done so. I set her breakfast tray down on the table that stood beside her bed, and she picked up the paper, and, of course, saw at once the paragraph I had just read, conspicuous on the front page under its headline 'Famous American Hostess Leaves London For New York.'

Miss Cornish read it through once or twice. Then, laying the paper down, she told me to bring her writing case from the drawing-room. She did not touch her breakfast, but when she rang for me to take the tray out two letters were lying on it, one addressed to Mr. Robinson, and the other to Mr. Mario. It did not surprise me to see the letter to Mario, I'd expected that, but I wondered at first what she was writing to Mr. Robinson about. Then I remembered that she was supposed to be having supper with him after the show that night, and I concluded that she'd put him off so that she could see Mario again and have things out with him. She told me to hurry and catch the early morning post so that they would be sure to be delivered that afternoon—she'd marked them both 'Urgent' on the envelopes—posts were quicker and better in those days than they are now, for all we're living in the atomic age. I took the letters and caught the post with them, but I wished with all my heart that I needn't have done so. I felt in my bones that they would only mean more trouble—as indeed they did, as events were to prove before that day was out.

CHAPTER ELEVEN

THE END OF A CHAPTER

MISS CORNISH had a lunch engagement that day with some young lord or other, and however bad she might have felt she pulled herself together to keep it. I couldn't help thinking how lovely she looked in her newest frock of pale grey foulard, dotted with pink spots, and a huge picture-hat of grey satin straw laden with pink roses on her blonde hair. I persuaded her to drink a glass of port wine before she left for her appointment, to brace her up a bit—she had been looking so white with all the worrying she'd been doing over that hateful fiddler of hers—and it had brought the colour back into her cheeks. And that was the last time I saw her look like that, young and gay and pretty—my poor, foolish, loving girl!

She stayed out all the afternoon, and I wasn't surprised at that for I knew that Mr. Mario was engaged all day with his agent so that she wouldn't be able to see him until after the show that night. And before she got back, there came a ring at the door, and when I went down to open it, there was Mr. Robinson on the doorstep! He looked as black as thunder and barked out: 'Your mistress in?' instead of saying 'Good day' to me as he usually did, for though I didn't much like him, he was a pleasant gentleman enough. When I said 'No, sir, not yet,' he grunted and pushed by me and strode into the drawing-room, banging the door behind him, obviously in a towering temper. My heart sank for poor Miss Cornish when she should come in.

She came about a quarter of an hour later, with the young lord. She made as if she intended to bring him in, but I shook my head and frowned at her and motioned towards the drawing-room, and she understood at once. She sent the young man away. Then, as the door closed behind her, she looked at me apprehensively.

'What is it?' she asked, and when I said 'Mr. Robinson's here, Miss,' she gave a little startled gasp.

'He's very upset about something,' I told her in a whisper. 'I think it's your letter. Oh, Miss, whatever did you say in it?'

'I can't imagine,' she said uncertainly. 'I only wrote putting him off our supper to-night after the show. I had to! I simply *must* see Mario, and to-night's my only chance.'

She unpinned her hat and handed it to me,

together with her handbag and gloves and the feather boa that all the ladies wore in those days, drew a deep breath and marched into the drawing-room, closing the door. I ran upstairs and put her things away, then, I must confess, I crept down again and listened at the door, I was so anxious to know what was happening. The door had come open a wee bit, the latch never caught properly unless it was slammed, so I was able to hear everything that went on—and what I heard sent my heart down into my boots with fear and concern.

What do you think that poor, foolish girl had done? Put the two letters she had written into the wrong envelopes—and Mr. Robinson had received the letter she had intended for Mario! And in it she'd given away everything! Her love affair with the violinist, her passion for him, her determination of going with him to America, and—worst of all!—she'd written some dreadfully slighting things about Mr. Robinson! She said that she had had enough 'of the love-making of that fat old pig,' and couldn't stand any more of it—enough to make any man mad. After all, it wasn't *his* fault if he was fat and bald and elderly—and he had been very generous to her, and I believe was really in love with her, though he couldn't marry her, for he had a wife already.

My! That was a scene! He stormed and swore, called her a bitch and a whore and goodness knows what else, and wouldn't listen to her when she tried to explain—though really it wasn't possible to explain anything, the truth was out and couldn't be denied! Then he started cursing Mario, and she lost her temper, too, and flared out at him, screaming that she loved Mario and was going to America with him to start a new life, and lots more like that. At last, he swung round on his heel and made for the door, telling her over his shoulder that he was through with her. Her allowance would be stopped from that day, and if she wasn't out of the flat in a week's time, he'd send the police and have her kicked out. She could get her fiddler to keep her and her brat!

I had only just time to whisk into the kitchen before he came storming out and dashed away, and I went into the drawing-room to find Miss Cornish with her cheeks the colour of the red carnations which had been Mr. Robinson's present to her the day before, and her blue eyes gleaming with anger. She was pouring herself out a glass of whisky and soda, and as I came in she drank it off in one draught, and then dumped the glass down so hard that it broke.

'Well, Skivvy,' she said. 'I've no doubt you heard it all. So that's over—and I'm glad of it!'

'So am I, miss,' I said, going on my knees to gather up the bits of glass that were scattered on the carpet. 'If you'll forgive the liberty, miss, I never have liked your knowing Mr. Robinson.'

'Oh, you're too respectable to live, Skivvy,' she said, but her tone wasn't unkind as she said it. 'Now I'm free and Mario's *got* to take me with him. He can't do anything else,' she added triumphantly, and again my heart sank. For I wondered. Miss Cornish as a mistress, with a luxurious flat and lots of drinks and good food handy, was one thing. But Miss Cornish without a penny, with a child into the bargain, would be a burden that that young man wouldn't be at all anxious to carry, unless I missed my guess.

But it was almost time for Miss Cornish to go to the theatre—and, anyway, it was no business of mine. So I helped her dress and saw her drive away in her brougham—the brougham that wouldn't be hers any more after next week. And then I gave Miss Marianne her supper and put her to bed, and settled down with my sewing to await Miss Cornish's return after the show.

When it was nearly time for her to come, I arranged a nice little supper for her and her lover on a little silver table in the drawing-room. As I set out the glass and silver I wondered afresh how my mistress would fare at the hands of the Italian when she broke the news to him. My heart was full of foreboding, which didn't decrease when he arrived— again before Miss Cornish—looking almost as black as Mr. Robinson had looked earlier. He almost threw his hat at me when I opened the door, and strode into the sitting-room, and I sighed to myself as I went upstairs to my room again. It was obvious that he had received the letter meant for Mr. Robinson, and had guessed what had happened.

After I heard Miss Cornish come in, I stole downstairs again to listen. I know I should not have done it, but I could not help myself—I simply *had* to know Mario's reaction. It was even worse than I had feared. Mario was in a frightful rage. He denounced Miss Cornish for every kind of fool that he could think of. Why in creation, he howled at her, had she done such a daft thing as mix up the letters, and lose a gold-mine like that fat ass, Robinson? She'd never find a richer one—and the best thing she could do now, would be to grovel to him and implore him to take her back. What did she think she would do without someone like him behind her? And if she thought that he, Mario, was going to take on the responsibility of looking after her and her damned child, she had better think again! His plans were made—he was off to New York next week—and nothing was going to stop him.

Here Miss Cornish interrupted his ravings, her voice so queer and hoarse that I hardly knew it for hers.

'And Lady Enderby? Is she going, too?'

He hesitated a moment, then he replied bluntly:

'Yes.'

'She's your mistress now, I suppose?' said Miss Cornish.

Again he hesitated, then again he answered bluntly:

'If you want the truth, yes! And I intend to get as much out of her as you've got out of Robinson.'

There was a long pause. Then his voice came again, conciliatory, almost carneying.

'Well, there it is, Gertie. Things had to come to an end between us, sometime. Surely you knew that?'

'I didn't! I—we talked of marriage—'

Mario made a sound of impatience.

'Talked! Talked! Who doesn't talk? Do be sensible, my dear girl! How on earth could I marry you even if you hadn't got a child? You haven't a bean—nor have I. It would be lunacy even to think of it! It's time to forget the nonsense we talked when we were in love. You be a wise girl and kowtow to Robinson. You know you can twist him round your little finger. And now wish me luck and let's part friends.'

There was no reply, and after a moment, Mario said snappishly:

'Well if you won't, you won't. I've done my best to talk sense into you, and I can't do more.'

I heard him move towards the door and I slipped silently back into the kitchen. Peeping through the crack of the kitchen door, I saw him come out of the drawing-room, pause and look back for a second, then snatch up his hat and go out into the night.

I waited a few minutes, then I went into the drawing-room. Miss Cornish was sitting staring before her like somebody in a trance. When I spoke to her, she gave a start and stared at me in a dazed way. I poured out a glass of wine and held it to her lips, and she

184

drank it. Then she came to herself and looked up at me, and I never saw eyes that wrung my heart more than hers did then!

'Dear Miss Gertie,' I said. And I could have broken down and cried to see the woe in her face. 'Let me pour you another—it'll help you to sleep.'

She held out her glass to be refilled.

'I shall need help to sleep to-night, Skivvy,' she said. 'You know what's happened? Mario's left me. All the plans we've made—the things we've talked of doing—marriage and a home together—all gone. Blown away like thistledown!'

I had her golden head cradled in my arms by this time, and was soothing her as I might have done a child. I hoped she would cry, for tears are an outlet—but she didn't. She just sobbed once or twice, then raised her head and got wearily to her feet.

'I'll go to bed now. While I'm undressing, Skivvy, run along to the chemist's and get some more of my sleeping tablets, there's a good girl. I've run out of them, and I simply *must* sleep to-night. The shop at the corner will still be open if you hurry.'

*   *   *

185

Looking back now, I suppose I ought to have suspected something, for it was only a few days since I'd bought the last lot of tablets for her. But I didn't. I did my errand and brought back a fresh bottle; one didn't have to have a doctor's prescription for them then. When I got back, Miss Cornish was already in bed, and she smiled at me faintly when I gave her the tablets, and told me to bring Miss Marianne down to spend the night with her in her bed. She often had the child to sleep with her when she was alone, so that didn't surprise me, and I went and carried the little thing down. She woke when I was laying her in her mother's bed and began to whimper, but Miss Cornish took her into her arms and began to pet her, and said to me over her shoulder.

'Go and make a pot of chocolate for her, will you, please, Skivvy?'

I hesitated for a moment.

'It's rather rich for her at this time of night. Wouldn't milk be better?' I asked. But she shook her head.

'No, she adores chocolate. Go and make it, there's a good girl.'

I went and made the chocolate and brought it in in a silver pot and a plate of sweet biscuits as well. I put two cups on the tray, though I'd noticed that Miss Cornish had brought a bottle of brandy and a glass up with her to her room. Still, I put the extra cup in case she'd take the hint, and said good night to them both. And that was the last time I ever saw either of them alive.

*   *   *

I found them when I went in quietly about nine o'clock the next morning, to take the child away from her mother, as I had so often done before. I think that when I opened the door of the darkened room, heavy with the odour of the scents and powders my poor, pretty girl used, I knew almost at once what had happened. There was such a silence, a dreadful heavy silence! I tore the window-curtains apart—and there they lay, mother and child, in each other's arms, as though they had fallen asleep together. As indeed they had, poor souls—but it was the sleep of death that had overtaken them.

I laid my hand on the child's arm, flung outside the crumpled silk coverlet, and it was cold as ice. As cold as the weight of fear and horror that fell on my heart at that moment. On the table beside the bed were two envelopes. One was addressed to me, the other to

187

Mr. Mario. She must have scribbled them after I had left the room, while she was waiting for the tablets to take effect, maybe after she had put her child to sleep with those devilish things—now I knew why she wanted the chocolate! The rich sweet taste would disguise any unpleasant flavour the tablets might have had, and the child adored chocolate—she would drink any amount. I picked up the letters, though my hand shook as though I had the ague, and I felt sort of dazed and couldn't think quite straight. Then, somehow I pulled myself together, and drew the curtains close again so that people might think she was sleeping late. And I put the letters in my pocket and went softly out of the room. There was no doubt in my mind as to whom I must go—Monsieur! I got my hat and coat and ran down the stairs and out along the streets until I reached his studio, praying all the while that he might be there, and not, as he was sometimes, sketching out in the country or staying at some client's house painting a portrait.

My luck was in. He was there. He was up and dressed and just drinking a cup of coffee when I rushed in, flung myself down on the divan and burst into tears. Much alarmed—for he had never before seen me anything but staid and conventional—he raised me on to the pillows and made me drink some of the coffee. Then he listened soberly as I poured out my tragic tale. At the finish, he nodded his head sadly.

'Ah! It is as I feared. Alas, she loved too much, *la pauvre*! But to take her life and that of the little one, also—ah, what a tragedy! What a tragedy, indeed!'

I drew a long breath. The relief of telling him and the hot strong coffee had pulled me together after a fashion, and I looked at him appealingly.

'I suppose I really ought to have gone first to the police,' I said. 'But somehow I wanted to ask you—'

'The police?' He looked quickly at me. 'Yes, the police must be told, but first we must think—think how we can perhaps save this poor one from some of the consequences of her folly. You are sure that she took her life and that of the child? It was not an accident?'

'No, I'm sure it wasn't an accident,' I said. 'If it had been an accident, she wouldn't have left the letters, would she?'

'No, she would not,' said Monsieur decisively. 'So we must see what she has written in those letters, my child—even in the letter she wrote for her lover. We can steam it open—then we can reseal it if it seems right

189

he should have it.'

'Oh, but, surely we can't do that?' I said. 'It's meant for him—it's private.'

'And is he, this Mario, so worthy a fellow that he must be considered?' asked Monsieur drily. 'You do not realize the position, my child. If your fear is true and she has left this letter to prove that she took her life, what scandal! What headlines in the papers to shock and distress any friends and relations she may have who love her! And more than that. There will be an inquest, you know, to find out how she died—and if it is proved that she took her own life and that of her child, they will be separated in death. For the one will be buried in consecrated ground—the other not.'

'Oh, no!' I cried out in horror. 'Surely they would bury them both together?'

Monsieur shook his head.

'No. Your poor, pretty Miss Cornish would be accounted a murderess and a suicide, and such are not allowed to rest in sacred ground. But before we talk any more, let us see what she has said in her letters.'

I opened my letter and he steamed open Mario's, and when we had read them we sat back and looked at each other.

'One thing is plain, Madame Emilie,'

190

Monsieur said at length. 'If we hope to have this poor girl buried in holy ground with her child in her arms, we must suppress these letters. In both of them, you see, she declares her determination to kill herself and her child, since without her lover there is nothing left for her in life and she cannot go without her little girl. So it must be done.'

I handed him my letter, though I would have given a lot to keep it. It was short and, oh, so sad—but it said how fond she was of me, and how much she appreciated what I'd tried to do for her and the child. And at the end she said what I valued more than anything else—that I was one of her few true friends. But I could see that it was impossible to keep it, so I gave it to Monsieur and watched him burn both letters to ashes in the stove.

'That is the most important thing done,' he said. 'Now the police must be told and her doctor called, and this lies in your hands, my child. You must not make a mistake over any point, for if they get suspicious the truth may yet be discovered in spite of our destroying the letters. You are sure nobody saw you leaving the house?'

'I'm sure,' I said. 'There was nobody about, and our next-door neighbour has gone down into the country to nurse a sick friend. And anyway, if anyone saw me they'd only think I'd gone to do the shopping early before Miss Cornish was up, as I often do.'

'Good. Now you must go back, and remember, however difficult it may be, for her sake you must act, act, act! Go into her room, open the curtains, and then throw open the window and call out as though in panic to the men in the mews—there are sure to be some there, are there not, getting the carriages ready for the day's work? Tell them to get the doctor. Say you can't wake your mistress and are frightened, but don't let anyone into the house until the doctor comes. When he comes, he will tell the police.'

He helped me to my feet, and said pityingly:

'I wish I could come with you and help you, but I dare not. It would cause such comment. I will support and advise you all I can, but it must be from the background, at least until all this is passed.'

'What will they do after the doctor has been?' I asked. 'Take her—them—away, I suppose, but what's to happen to all her things? Must I stay there—alone—to take care of them?'

'Ask the police to keep guard over the flat

while you are there alone, for fear lest thieves break in,' Monsieur told me. 'She had furs and jewellery, had she not, worth money? I fear you will have to stay there for the present. You were her trusted maid, remember, and until you are relieved of the charge you are still responsible for her things. But do not fear—I will not be far off—and if you have courage all will be well.'

NOTE BY SALLIE STILWELL

Here came another of the gaps in Skivvy's story. A whole handful of pages was missing, and of others only bits remained. By patiently piecing the readable fragments together, we made out enough, however, to give us an idea of what must have happened after Skivvy called the police.

Apparently an old aunt who had brought Miss Cornish up appeared on the scene and took charge of the flat and her niece's things. She seems not to have been too pleasant to Skivvy, probably thinking that she had encouraged her niece in her erring ways, and there was one page, clear enough to read, which told of a scene where the aunt was so nasty that the poor girl wept and went off and took refuge with Monsieur—which no doubt confirmed the aunt's opinion that she was no better than she should have been!

The next really readable portion of the manuscript was Skivvy's description of the time when she was before the Coroner, being asked questions about her mistress's death:

I clenched my hands together and stared at him, trying to remember the instructions Monsieur had given me.

'Answer briefly and speak up. Don't go into long descriptions. Don't mention anybody's name. If you are pressed, just say you minded your own business and did not inquire into your mistress's affairs.' I heard the Coroner speak.

'Did you ever hear your mistress talk of ending her life?'

'No, sir.' In this at least I did not have to lie. Until she found her lover false, life had tasted good to Gertie Cornish, and the last thing she would ever have thought of was death. The Coroner went on:

'Did you know anything in your mistress's life that could have led her into wanting to take it? A broken love affair? Disappointment in her professional life? Anything like that?'

'No, sir,' I said. But the man was pressing me.

'Come, come! You were living with this lady, seeing her friends, knowing what she did. Do you mean to tell me that she never had any quarrels with any of her—admirers?'

'If she did, sir, I didn't hear them,' I said steadily.

My questioner looked unbelieving.

'But you were living in the same flat. You *must* have heard something of what went on.'

'The flat was on two floors, sir, and I was mostly with the child on the upper floor. I didn't hear much of what went on below.'

The man who was questioning me looked sideways at me and I could see he didn't believe me.

'Your mistress was a very pretty woman,' he said. 'She must have had many admirers. Can you remember her seeing one man in particular more often than the others?'

I gripped the rail of the stand on which I stood. Now I knew I must be very careful, for, as Monsieur had pointed out, it was no use now that the poor girl was dead in blackening her memory or in dragging the names of the men in her life into the open. 'Be as vague and non-committal as possible,' Monsieur had told me, and I answered as he had directed.

'She had many friends, sir, both gentlemen and ladies, but I couldn't say which of them were her special favourites.'

He frowned at me.

'Oh, come now, Mrs. Bligh! You aren't going to deny that there was one man in particular of whom Miss Cornish saw a great deal. Signor Mario Buonalozzi, for instance, who, we know, visited her frequently, and who is now, I understand, in America? Might it not have been distress at his departure that caused her to take her life?'

'Mr. Mario was one of her great friends, I know,' I said. 'He played at the theatre where she acted, and she thought he was a wonderful fiddler. It was through her he got to know—' for the fraction of a second Lady Enderby's name was on my tongue. Then I remembered Monsieur's 'No names!' and went on—'the gentleman who arranged for him to go to America.'

That was true at all events! It had been through her, indirectly, that he had got to know Mr. Solomons.

'Very altruistic of her,' commented my interrogator, in a sneering way that put my back up and made me retort:

'Anyway, the night he went to America she was laughing and playing with her little girl as usual, so it doesn't look as though she was heart-broken, does it, sir?'

196

There was a little stir in court and I knew I'd made a useful point. The Coroner switched the questions to the child. Was she an inquisitive child? The kind of child who might, when her mother's back was turned, poke her fingers into the bottle that contained the tablets and taste them, thinking they were sweets? I said yes to that, for indeed it was true. Miss Marianne was forever after sweet-stuffs, wheedling one into buying goodies for her, or prying round to see what she could find.

'Was your mistress in the habit of taking sleeping tablets?' I didn't like the word 'habit,' and I replied to that question very cautiously.

'Well, sir, she did take them sometimes. She took them when she couldn't settle down to sleep easily—times when she was working extra hard and was overtired and wasn't sleeping well. That week she had been rehearsing for a new play as well as doing her usual turns, and I know she was feeling the strain a little.'

That, too, was true, and the Coroner nodded and played with his pencil. I looked at him anxiously and decided that, on the whole, he had a kindly face. Somehow, it seemed to me, in spite of his searching questions, he didn't want to give a verdict of suicide, and would welcome a chance of avoiding it if possible.

I brought my thoughts back with a jerk, for he was speaking again.

'Do you think it possible that your mistress might already have taken her usual dose of sleeping pills and then forgotten that she had done so, and taken the dose again? Was she a forgetful person?'

I pounced eagerly on this opening.

'Oh, yes, sir! She was dreadfully forgetful. She's asked me more than once if I could tell her if she'd taken this or that medicine or something, because she couldn't remember if she had.'

'Ummm,' said the Coroner. 'Well, gentlemen, from what we have heard of this unfortunate young lady there really seems no reason why she should commit suicide. She had a pleasant home which was apparently her own so long as she chose to occupy it.' I breathed a sigh of relief. Evidently no hint of Mr. Robinson's break with her had leaked out, nor even a hint of their relationship—though I heard afterwards that this had only been avoided by bribery on the part of Mr. Robinson. 'She had a pleasant home, she had plenty of friends, had no need of money, was appearing in a successful show and rehearsing for its successor. She had a child to whom she was devoted. So far as I can see, nothing has been disclosed about her life that should have given her any reason to wish to end it.'

The verdict, thank God, was 'Accidental Death.' It was decided that Miss Cornish had taken a second dose of sleeping tablets, forgetting that she had already taken a heavy dose. And that her child, playing around in the bed, had seen her mama taking them, and had swallowed some herself when her mother's attention was temporarily distracted. So they were safe! They could lie together, now, quietly sleeping, in consecrated ground, and nobody could point a finger of scorn at my poor, pretty girl who had died for love of a worthless man.

I don't remember exactly what happened after the verdict had been pronounced. I heard a murmur go round the court and knew that it was a sound of sympathy, and then I came over all queer and giddy. Someone, I don't know who, helped me down some steps and sat me in a chair, and somebody else brought water, and then a hand, strong, and kind, and comforting, took mine, and I clung to it blindly.

After awhile, I managed to pull myself together, and looked up to see who the hand belonged to. And, of course, it was Monsieur! He had been at the back of the court room all the time, though he had not let me see him for fear of distracting me.

'You did wonderfully, *mon enfant*,' he said, and as I looked into his kind eyes, I wondered how I could ever have thought him queer or ugly. 'You did wonderfully well. But now you are exhausted and need looking after, and so you are coming home with me.'

CHAPTER TWELVE

MONSIEUR

So THAT was how my life with Monsieur began.

I did not go to him as a mistress—sex at that time simply did not enter into our relationship. It was never even in our thoughts. Yet that was, of course, considered to be my position by the world at large. Although he was many years my senior, that made no difference. Had I visited him daily as his servant, it would have been all right—I would have been looked upon merely as his maid. Perhaps it would have been wiser if I had found a room outside where I could sleep. But there it was, I didn't and it never occurred to Monsieur to worry about the opinion of the world. So, after the inquest, back we went to the studio, and I was so exhausted with emotion and excitement that I collapsed on the divan and went fast off to sleep.

I slept for many hours and when I awoke it was night-time, and there was a delicious smell of coffee in the air, and in the corner by the stove Monsieur was making an omelette. I blinked and sat up, but the little man looked at me and shook his head vigorously.

'Lie still, Emilie,' he ordered—'You do not realize, my child how great a shock you have received. Now it is all over, and you must rest for awhile, and after that you must try to put it behind you—to look ahead and not behind, as you are too fond of doing.'

There was meaning in his tone. Though he knew much about my early life, I had never told him about Birdie, but he was quite shrewd enough to guess that there were pages in that life I had not let him read, though he never asked questions. He brought a tray over to me in a few minutes, on which was the omelette and a slice of bread-and-butter, and watched with pleasure as I sat up and began to eat hungrily. While I ate, he continued talking.

'Now you must make a new life for yourself, and till then you must stay here, rest and eat well, and sleep as much as you can, and talk nonsense with your friend Monsieur. Then when those big dark circles round your eyes have gone, and you have got back the weight you have lost and have learnt to laugh again, then we will think about getting you another job. *When* you are fit for one, which at the moment, *petite*, you are not.'

'I'm afraid,' I said, with a spurt of bitterness, 'that having to appear in court about this case won't help me to get another post. Ladies don't like girls who have been in the papers, or girls who've been maid to anyone like poor Miss Cornish.'

'Women!' said Monsieur contemptuously. 'I know—she was *une femme entretenue*, and they would say "Like mistress, like maid." Well, we will talk about that when you are strong again, and meantime you must stay here.'

'I've no money,' I said doubtfully. 'Not even my last week's wages. She forgot to pay me—and food and light cost money and—'

He interrupted me with a little sound of impatience.

'*Tiens*, that obstinate pride of yours! If you must measure up what I do for you with what you do for me—well, you can clean and tidy this room, can you not? And you can wash whatever needs washing, and shop, and write my letters for me—I, who write the most execrable English! And who knows, after a time I might even let you do some cooking, though I have never met an English woman yet who could cook as I can!'

That last was true. He could have earned big money as a chef, could my Monsieur. He

203

was the most wonderful cook I ever came across.

What he said comforted me a good deal. So I began my new life, and when the time came that I had recovered and was my energetic self again, I had got so used to that life and was so happy in it, that even if a good job had come along, I am sure I should never have taken it.

But no good job, or, indeed, any job, came along. I had been right—ladies would have nothing to do with a girl who had been mixed up in a case such as poor Miss Cornish's. Besides, I had no references, and hadn't a chance of getting one. I visited one or two registry offices, and answered a number of advertisements by ladies wanting maids, but though one or two of them asked me to call and see them, none of them would even consider me once they found that I couldn't give a reference. One lady recognized my name from having read about the inquest, and started to ask me inquisitive questions about my poor girl, and I revolted and answered her rudely, and, of course, quickly found myself outside the door.

It was that night that Monsieur came in and found me crying forlornly beside the fire. I hadn't expected him back so soon, for he had gone down to the 'Club Francais,' where he met his cronies and smoked and played cards and talked of the beloved France. But that night he came in early, bringing a chicken and a bottle of wine, and a yard of fresh bread, one of the long French rolls which he always bought if he could get them.

'We are going to have a feast,' he announced as he came into the studio. We will have *pain grille* to eat with our chicken, and a beautiful bottle of Bordeaux to drink. And see—this is for my little Emmee who does so much to keep my attic bright and clean.'

It was a spray of moss roses. He tossed it into my lap and for a moment I looked at it dumbly. It was a lovely thing, a single spray of tiny red moss rosebuds, with a bit of white jasmine and a scrap of fern to set them off. The sight and the smell of it, and the kindness of its giver, overcame me completely, and bowing my head over it, I burst into fresh and bitter tears.

Alarmed, Monsieur fell on his knees at my side, and drawing me tenderly into his arms begged me to tell him what was wrong. Sobbing like a baby, I told him how impossible it was to find employment and how worried I was at living with him like that and as to what I ought to do. He heard me out in silence, and when I had sobbed and talked myself into a comparative quietness, he put me back into my chair, and drew his own up beside me. His face was grave, and he took my hand between both his own and held it while he talked.

'So this is why my little Emmee has been so moody these last few weeks. Listen to me, and know that I do not wish to persuade you to stay with me against your will—though if you leave me now, I shall miss you more than you can ever know. It is true that the world will think, as you fear, that we are living in sin, but who now is left in the world for whose opinion you care? Your grandmother is dead, and you have broken away from the friends you knew in your youth—so why should you care for the opinion of the world outside?'

He looked down at my hand and stroked it gently as he went on:

'See here, my Emmee. If I could offer you marriage I would do so—but alas, I cannot! I have told you of my desolation when I lost my Simone, but what I did not say was that in my madness I became entangled with a woman. I took her as one takes a drug, hoping that it would kill the pain for awhile, and when she told me that she was *enceinte* I believed her and I married her. Then I found that she had lied to me and there was no child, and we quarrelled bitterly, and at last I left her, and where she is living now I do not know. So, even if you were willing to consider marriage with an ugly little fellow so many years your senior, I could not offer it—much as I should like to.'

I was so astonished, and so touched, that I didn't know what to say, and after a moment or two he went on:

'So all I can do is to say to you, "Stay here as long as you will, my dear, and go on seeking a post that will suit you." Something may come along. I will light a candle for you to our Lady of Pity, and we will pray together, you in your way and I in my way, wicked little Papist that I am, that you may find a job that you will like and be happy in.'

Something caught at my throat, and I said, jerkily:

'I shall never be as happy anywhere, as I am here.'

There was a long pause, and then Monsieur spoke slowly:

'You mean that, despite what the world will say, despite my poverty and my age, and everything else—you would rather stay here with me than go elsewhere?'

'Yes,' I whispered—for then I knew the truth. Nothing mattered for me now but to stay with Monsieur—the kindest, truest man

I had met since Johnny's death, the sweetest, gentlest man I was ever to meet. Slowly he rose to his feet and laid his hands on my shoulders, pulling me up to face him, and his was grave.

'Think, my child, think. I would not have you live to regret this moment in a later, saner, mood. You are still young—many years younger than I am—'

'I know,' I said. 'But I'm old enough to know what things are worth having and what are not. I was a fool to worry about what people might say. What does it matter? All I know is that you have given me rest and peace and kindness and comfort and that I can't imagine life without you.'

His arms went round me then, at first hesitatingly, then with a warmth and a passion wonderful to me, who had been for so long lonely and unwanted. His voice in my ear came to me like music.

'Oh, *mon amour*—my little one whom I have loved so long and dared not show it. Yes, ever since the day you first brought the child to sit for me. You are young and comely, and I a man nearly old enough to be your father, poor and ugly and without a decent home to offer you—and yet you think that you can love me?'

I nodded my head, voiceless, and for a moment we stood together, held close in each other's arms. Then he gently lifted my chin and kissed me on the lips—a lingering, wonderful kiss, a kiss to remember, as, indeed, I remember it now. Then, releasing me, he turned to the table on which he had laid his purchases, once more the practical Frenchman.

'So here, without knowing it, I have brought our wedding breakfast! Turn on the lamp, *mon chou*, and I will cook you a chicken better than any you have ever tasted before. While I do it, you will put on your best dress, for this is our wedding night. And when all is ready I will put on the velvet coat I keep to impress the ladies that I am a real artist, and we will eat and drink to our future together—Monsieur and Madame Monsieur!'

* * *

It is strange how quickly one gets to accept as normal, something one has been taught to believe is wrong! Though for a little while I felt shy and awkward and guilty after I had decided to go on living with Monsieur, it was odd how soon I got used to being his—no, I won't write mistress! He was always so angry when I called myself that, though, of course, it was true. I was his *wife*, he said, and all his friends would understand and treat me as such, and though at first I had difficulty in believing that, I realized after awhile that it was true.

Maybe it was because most of his friends were foreigners, and foreigners don't seem to look at these things in the way that we do. Partly, perhaps, it was because they were mostly men. Women might have been less friendly, though I'm bound to say that the few I met were always friendly enough.

Monsieur wanted me to learn French, so that I could join in the conversation when his friends came to see him. The idea dismayed me at first, but he was very firm, and when I came to think about it, it seemed to me that he was in the right of it. To have linked up my life with a Frenchman, to play hostess to his friends, and yet never to learn his language would have been not only rude, but silly, for certainly life would be less dull for me if I could understand what they were jabbering about, these cheerful, friendly foreigners who so often climbed the long stairs to the studio for coffee and for the talk that seemed to be the very breath of life to them. So he began to teach me, and I think perhaps I had a sort of aptitude for languages, for in a surprisingly short time I found myself with quite a respectable vocabulary of nouns. Verbs, Monsieur said, could come afterwards, and he was quite right, for once I had learnt the words for food and clothes and essential things like that, the verbs to link them up seemed to just come along and fit in. Monsieur was very pleased at my progress, and when I had got a stumbling kind of grasp of the language, he took to talking only French to me at meals, and gradually I became able both to speak and understand it. I was never very good at it, of course, but I could follow more or less what Monsieur and his friends were saying, and could even take a small part in their conversation myself, though often my hearers would be convulsed with laughter at the mistakes I made.

While I was studying French, I also learnt to write—I mean not just the kind of writing I'd learnt in school, but the kind educated people wrote, the kind that enabled me to put into writing all the things I wanted to say. That was really useful, for Monsieur hated writing letters and always put off answering those he received as long as he possibly could. After a bit, I took to answering them for him, and I also dealt with his bills and things of that sort. I found a tangle of papers stuffed into drawers and boxes all over the studio, and some of the letters ought to have been answered ages ago. Among the tangle I found quite a number of cheques that he had never even bothered to cash, though none of them big, as his work wasn't fetching then the prices it did after he died, poor darling. But there were a sufficient number to add up to quite a respectable sum, and when they were all cashed, I found we were much better off than I had imagined.

After all the publicity about Miss Cornish's death, some of the newspapers remembered what a success the portrait of her little girl had been, and mentioned the name of the artist who had painted it. That resulted in quite an uprush of interest in Monsieur and his work, and several really worthwhile commissions came along that delighted us both. Monsieur made me pay all the money we could save into my Savings Account in the Post Office. I demurred about it a bit, but he insisted, and long afterwards I understood why he was so determined that I should build up a little nest egg, to have something to fall back upon in case of illness or a blank patch with no money coming in.

Oh, they were happy years, those years with Monsieur—the happiest time, I think, of all my life! It was during them that I started writing this story. Monsieur was so interested in the things I told him about my early life, the English countryside, the food, the customs, that he wanted me to write them down. They were worth remembering, he said, and might even make a book, a real book that would be printed and sell and make us a lot of money. I laughed at that and didn't believe it, but he was so good to me that I'd have done anything to please him. So I started to write, and soon I found it so interesting to put my thoughts and my memories down on paper that I've gone on writing ever since. Monsieur used to make me read over to him the bits I'd written, and he would point out where I'd gone wrong in grammar or punctuation or things like that. Though he hated writing in English, he was a wonderful judge of good writing through his reading, and he often made me alter the wording of my story, so as to make it sound better. Of course, when I was writing it at first, I left out all about Birdie. I couldn't bear Monsieur to know about that, though, as things worked out, he had to know it all in the end.

Yes, we were very happy together, my little Monsieur and I, in those years when King Edward VII was on the throne, and everything was gay and nobody guessed all that was to come. It would take too long to put down all I remembered about them, and it might be boring as well, so I shall go on to something that happened that shook my life to its very foundations—I met Birdie again.

It happened in this way. There was a big Exhibition at Shepherds Bush called the White City, and when it was opened, all London, and half the country as well, crowded to it. There were miles and miles of shining white buildings in the most fantastic shapes, Oriental Style, people said it was, all domes and pinnacles and balconies and colonnades. In the middle there was a big lake one could go boating on in pretty painted boats, and there were shops and booths and roundabouts, and places where you could shoot or throw things for prizes. The most astonishing thing of all was a kind of gigantic thing they called the Great Wheel, or the Flip-Flap. It was an enormous wheel with a lot of little cages hung on it, full of people, and when the wheel turned the cages went up with it and the people in them could see over the White City, and for miles over London as well. There were always crowds waiting to go up in it, though I never wanted to. I'd have been scared to death! And before the end of the season there'd been one or two times when the mechanics had gone wrong, and the people in the cages had been stuck up there for hours, so I think I was right not to go.

Monsieur took me first to the White City at night, and it was lovely. There was a band playing, and one could dance, and all the buildings were outlined with fairy lights, and there was a cascade that poured down into the lake over some glass steps, and there were lights behind the steps that shone through the falling water and kept on changing. You never saw anything so lovely in your life. I enjoyed it so much that I decided to go again, in daylight. I knew Monsieur had arranged to go painting in the country with some of his friends one day, so I dropped a card to a friend of mine, Letitia Bourne, suggesting that she should meet me—it was her day off—and we'd go together to the White City and spend the afternoon there. Letitia had been one of the maids at Mrs. Fortescue's, and she had always kept up with me, for she knew that the affair with Mr. Arnold hadn't been my fault. She was delighted with the idea, and she was enchanted with it all when we got there. We wandered about enjoying ourselves, and went on one or two of the mechanical things, though not the Great Wheel! and tried our luck in the shooting gallery, and bought a few oddments from the booths and stalls. By the time we'd bought all we could afford and had had ices in a pretty little restaurant it was getting late, so I said to Letitia that I thought we had better leave, and as she agreed we began to make our way back to the entrance.

To get to the entrance we had to pass by the big lake, and we stopped for a few minutes to watch the boats on the water. As we stood watching, I felt a touch on my elbow, and when I turned round to see who it was, there, of all people, was my lady, with Lord Stilwell beside her, smiling down at me!

'Why Emily! How very nice to run into you like this,' she said. 'And how well you're looking!' She held out her hand to me and I took it dumbly. For the moment I was so astonished that I couldn't think of anything to say. But she went on talking, as kind and sweet-smiling as she always was to me, my dear lady! And I managed after awhile to stammer out something about how glad I was to see her, but what it was I hardly knew at the time, I was so busy staring at her.

She had changed very little, I thought, in the past ten years, and was still as lovely as ever, though of course in an older and more sophisticated way. She was plying me with questions, and I had to pull myself together and answer them. Where was I living now? Was I working for anyone, or had I married again? She did so hope I had—I was so young to be a widow. She had been so sorry, so very sorry for my loss.

For a second I hesitated—then I uttered the necessary lie. After all, when one burns one's boats one might as well burn them completely!

'Yes, my lady, I'm married again. To—to an artist, and very happily, My name, now is Madame Yvetôt.'

Lady Stilwell smiled with pleasure and patted my shoulder. A breath of the delicate perfume she used came to me, and just for a moment I could have closed my eyes and gone back through the years to the time when I was little Emily Skeffington, tweeny-maid at the Manor.

'I *am* glad,' she said. 'And to an artist— how interesting. I can see you're happy, and I am so pleased to meet you again.' Her eyes were on Letitia, whom I hastily presented, and she went on:

'Isn't this Exhibition wonderful? I think this lake is the best part of it. Such a draw, too. There's my Freddie, just coming back from his third trip. He's sixteen years old now, you know. Not a little boy any longer.'

'Is he—is he well, my lady?' I ventured.

'Oh, he's always well, bless him,' said my lady. 'Look, there he is, just coming off the boat now.'

Feeling as though I were living in some strange dream, I watched the passengers coming off the boat that had just drawn in to the landing-place. Yes, I could see him! He was with two other young folk, his cousins, I felt sure. They were all handsome young people but to my eyes there was no comparison between them. My Birdie was the tallest and handsomest of all. He was tanned with the sun and he still had those starry blue eyes—I saw them as he lifted his head to smile at my lord and lady. My heart went out towards him in a great wave of emotion as he pushed his way through the throng and came to Lady Stilwell's side. My lady put her hand on my arm and drew me forward.

'Here is somebody whom you won't remember, Freddie,' she said. 'This is Emily, who used to work at the Manor House and who often nursed you when you were a baby.'

He held out his hand with a boyish grin, and I took it in mine and looked into the friendly depths of those speedwell-coloured eyes. There was no recognition in them—how

218

could there be when he had only seen me once when he was a child of three? Yet, foolishly, I felt that I must do something to recall myself to his memory, and a recollection shot into my mind.

'There's one thing you may perhaps remember, sir,' I said, and was surprised to find my voice quite steady and normal. 'You were only three when I saw you last, but when I picked you up you snatched at a green beetle that was in my hat and wouldn't let it go.'

He looked puzzled at first. Then suddenly his face lighted up and he looked at my lady and laughed.

'That green beetle! I remember it now. I had it for a long time, but I'd forgotten where it came from. I expect I was a spoilt brat! I'm awfully sorry if I damaged your hat.'

'You know, I really meant to return that beetle,' said my lady, ruefully. 'But he went to sleep with it clutched in his hand, and he wouldn't let it go out of his sight for days. And then I hadn't your address, and goodness knows what became of it in the end. And talking of addresses, you must really give me yours now. Freddie, have you got a pencil and anything on which to write?'

The boy shook his head, and my lord

laughed as he pulled out a pencil and an envelope and handed them to me.

'Pockets stuffed with everything in the world, except something that might be useful,' he remarked. 'Can you write your name and address on that, Mrs.—er—um? I'm afraid it's all I've got in the way of paper.'

I didn't really want to do it, but I didn't see how to avoid it, so I scribbled down my name and address on the envelope and handed it back. My lady had her hand now on Birdie's shoulder—and suddenly I felt such a wave of fury and jealousy that it quite startled me. It ought to have been *my* hand resting there. It ought to have been *my* right to ruffle that curly hair, to kiss that smooth sunburnt cheek, to go about with him at my elbow escorting me—the boy who was flesh of my flesh and bone of my bone.

I suppose that I made my *adieux* politely, though I had no recollection of having done until suddenly I realized that the Stilwells had gone and that Letitia and I were standing alone. She was staring at me curiously.

'Are you all right, Emily?' she asked.

'Of course I am,' I said, 'Why?'

'Oh, you struck me as a bit curt when your lady said good-bye to you, and you never answered when Master Freddie did. I must say he's got good manners, that boy. Took off his cap and bowed as though we were two of his mama's lady friends, instead of a couple of—'

'Skivvies!' I said bitterly. 'Come on, let's go home. It's late.'

We joined the crowds trailing towards the exit gates, and we had just reached them and were waiting our turn to file through when I was aware of a pair of sharp eyes staring at me. Dark eyes, set in a face plastered with powder and paint—Tilda, of all people!

She was with a stout middle-aged man, who was pressing forward a little ahead of her. I was conscious of Letitia's surprised face beside me. It was not difficult to see what type of woman poor Tilda was, and Letitia wouldn't be able to understand how I came to know such a person. Even though I wasn't married to Monsieur, my position was too high to stoop to *that* level. To see her again gave me a shock of dismay, but the crush was so great it was impossible to avoid her. She was pushed close against me by the crowd, and her breath smelt of drink as she spoke to me.

'Hey, Skivvy! You going to cut your old friend?' she grinned, and my revulsion must have shown in my face, for the grin took on a malicious twist.

'I was standing right by you over there while you were talking to the Stilwells—my lord and lady and their promising young son! What a fine-looking lad he is, isn't he? Not a bit like his father or his mother—isn't that odd? Could he be a sort of throwback, do you think, to one of his ancestors?'

She was talking close to my ear, and I could only pray that Letitia would not hear what she was saying. I was in a panic as to what she would let out, for it was plain she had had too much to drink. But, mercifully we came out close to the gate then, and as the crowd went streaming through, her escort caught her by the arm and hurried her off. She shouted at me over her shoulder as she was hustled away.

'So long, Skivvy! I'll come along and see you one of these days.'

Letitia looked at me as we emerged into the street.

'That woman! How does she come to know you?'

I told her briefly where I had met Tilda, and how sorry I was she had sunk to her present level.

'Oh, I see,' she said. 'But I'd avoid her now, if I were you, Emily. It's no credit to a decent woman to have her for a friend.'

'I'm not likely to see her again except by accident, like today,' I protested. 'She doesn't know where I live, thank goodness, so she can't hunt me out.'

'Well, that's a good thing,' said Letitia, as we parted to catch our different buses. 'If ever there was a nasty mischief in any woman's voice, it was in hers when she said she'd be seeing you.'

*   *   *

It was this meeting with my darling that brought about the disclosure of the truth to Monsieur—though actually it was not really news to him—he knew already that I had had a child. It came about, the disclosure, because when I got home and found that he had not returned from his painting expedition, I threw myself on the bed and gave way to a mad fit of jealousy against my lady. 'Oh, God!' I cried out—cried aloud in my anger. '*Why* should she have the right to have my child, to love him, and look after him, to pet him and kiss him. He's mine, mine, *mine*, and the whole world ought to know it!'

I clenched my fist and thumped the wall at the side of the bed, and sobbed aloud in sheer fury that I had not had the courage to keep my son, to keep him and love him and work for him, as braver women than I had done. I was so lost in the storm of furious emotion that I never heard Monsieur come in, and it was only when he sat down beside me that I realized he was there and must have heard what I was saying. His voice when he spoke was as gentle as though he were talking to a child.

'*Mon p'tit chou*, is it not time that you told me all about it?'

I mumbled something, I don't know what, and he went on:

'See, *mon enfant*, in everyone's life there is a secret garden into which nobody has the right to intrude. Sometimes that secret garden, into which we all retreat at times, brings peace and we emerge from it better and stronger, refreshed by our rest there. But you, my little one, do not find rest in your secret garden. That I have known for a long time.'

I could not face his deepset eyes, kind as they were. I looked down and fumbled at the fringe of the bedspread.

'I—I don't know what you mean,' I whispered.

There was an edge of sternness in his voice when he spoke again.

'I must be plain, then, my Emilie, for to

leave hidden any longer this secret that makes you unhappy is to let it grow into a canker, and that must not be. Now do not flinch from me, my dear one. I love you as you are, as I have always, and *shall* always, love you. What do I care what you have done in the past before we met? I have known for a long time that you have had a child that was not your husband's. Had it been you would have told me about it, as you have told me about the little girl that died.'

I drew my breath in sharply, I was so amazed, and he went on:

'I found it out by accident. Do you remember once how I came in earlier than usual and found you weeping by the fire? You said you had a bad headache and were feeling depressed, and I sent you off to bed for I feared that you might have caught the influenza of which there was an epidemic then. I thought to myself that I would give you one of those pain-killing tablets you sometimes take for headaches, but I could not find them, so I looked inside your handbag to see if they were there. And in the bag I found an envelope so worn with age that it opened as I took it out and I saw that there was a snapshot in it, a snapshot of a baby. And pinned to it was a little poem copied out in your handwriting.'

I was deathly silent, and he went on again:

'Now, my dear one, it is not normal for a young woman to keep with her always the photograph of somebody else's baby. To keep it so much with her, and to look at it so often, that the edges of the envelope where it lives are worn through with taking it in and out. Nor is it normal for her to copy out a poem such as this, to keep with the photograph. And he began to recite in a voice soft as a bird's at twilight:

Where did you come from, baby dear?
    'Out of the everywhere into here.'
Where did you get those eyes so blue?
    'Out of the sky as I came through.'
Where did you get that pearly ear?
    'God spoke, and it came out to hear.'
How did you get that dimpled cheek?
    'It came when I smiled to hear God
        speak.'
Where did you get that curling hair?
    'It stands for the halo the angels wear.'
Teeth, where did you come from, you dar-
        ling things?
    'From the same box as the cherubs'
        wings.'
How did it all just come to be you?

226

'God thought about me, and so I grew.'
And how did you come to us, you dear?
'God thought about you, and so I'm
here.'

I put out my arms to him, speechless, and
he lifted me up and held me close to his breast,
and for a wonderful moment we clung together, keyed up to a height of emotional
intensity that few people, I think, can ever
have experienced. If I had not known it before
I knew then that my little man was the nearest
thing to a saint I would ever have the chance
of knowing. And in my mind I begged God to
forgive me the mad, wicked things I had been
thinking and saying a few minutes ago, and to
let me thank Him, instead, for giving me the
love of this man who was so like what His own
Son must have been—gentle, understanding,
all-forgiving.

Sitting together afterwards in the yellow
lamplight, I showed Monsieur again the precious snapshot which Mrs. Dibben had once
sent me of my Birdie, and we read together
the poem I had remembered from my childhood and had written out because it said for
me so much that I couldn't say for myself.
And I told him all about Valentine, and what
Tilda and I had done with my baby. And as I

told my sordid little tale, his face darkened, and he caught me to him and held me close again.

'The vile one! *Le sacré cochon!*' he hissed. 'Oh, had I but been there I would have killed him before he should have touched you, my poor child! Big he may have been, but I was strong and these hands have done more damage in their time than I could, or ever would, tell you! Even now, it is better that I do not know where he lives. To rape a young thing, helpless, unable to defend herself—to do that when love should be learnt tenderly, kindly—not forced on youth before the time is ripe.'

He was angrier than I had ever seen him be before, but after a moment, he pulled himself together.

'Forgive me! It is not only jealousy that speaks. It offends something deep down in me to know that such a vile one, should have had the gift of your virgin body in all its freshness, all its beauty. But now, my love, you are a woman who is all mine—all, that is, but the part you give to this child of yours. Ah, God! Had it but been *my* child! How I would have cherished it, adored it, lived for it.'

I hid my face.

'Don't—oh, please don't hate me for

deserting it?' I whispered. 'I know I was a coward, but I was so afraid. I didn't dare face the world with a baby born that way.'

'Hate you? Ah, never, my dear one. You seized what chance offered you to do what seemed to you the best for your child, as well as for yourself. How should a child of sixteen find the courage to keep her baby, born out of wedlock, in the teeth of the world? I do not blame you, my Emmee, never, never! I do but offer my advice, to try to ease this thing a little for you. Try not to dwell too much on this child who is now heir to a famous name and the wealth that goes with it. You gave him up—and now, even in your mind, you must try to relinquish him in truth, wholly and completely. You know that he is with those who love him and are proud of him.'

'I know. But they love and are proud of a lie,' I muttered bitterly.

'For that you cannot blame them. Only be glad that your son is happy. Be glad of that— and try not to think of anything else. Put it all far back in your mind, and dwell in the present, where you live, my darling, with me.'

I smiled up at him. It was rather a watery smile, but it reassured him, and swinging, as he so often did, from seriousness to gaiety, he sprang suddenly to his feet.

'Emmee, Emilie—now I have the courage to ask you something I have not dared to ask before. You have a beautiful body—round, soft, dimpled, such as the master, Boucher, would have loved to paint. Let me paint you as I have seen you as a lover, naked and unashamed? Let me make you immortal, so that those who come after me when I am dead, coming across a picture of you, shall stare and wonder and say "Where *did* he find her, a woman with so beautiful a body?"'

* * *

And so I became my little man's model. I made two stipulations; one, that if I sat for him no other girl should do so, and, secondly, that when I was sitting the door should be always locked. He kept these promises faithfully.

I found it very hard at first to remain long in one position. But Monsieur was very patient with me, and the knowledge that I was saving him the cost of employing a professional model, spurred me on, so that, after awhile, he said that I was as good as any professional. The most trying part to me was the time it took up, the time which, before, I had been able to spend on my housekeeping, cleaning, shopping, cooking and so on. But when one has to, one can somehow arrange these things, and I contrived to plan my hours so that I was able to do all the sitting Monsieur needed and my housekeeping as well.

There was an exhibition of pictures given at a small picture gallery in Soho especially for foreign painters living in London, and though I was very reluctant about it, Monsieur insisted on sending to it a study he had done of me which he called *After the Bath*. It showed me sitting naked on the edge of the divan, drying my hair with a towel, with a heap of clothes beside me and the old dog lying on the top of them. It had been a dreadfully difficult pose to hold, for both my arms were raised to throw my breasts forward, but from the excited way Monsieur and his friends discussed it they evidently thought it was a fine study. The picture was sent into the show, and lo and behold!, it took first prize—a hundred pounds. And not only that—it meant a write-up in the papers, too, and that, in its turn, brought more money in the shape of fresh work. That year my little Monsieur was kept really busy, and our little nest egg grew.

At that point there came another break in Skivvy's MS, a really bad one this time. A whole mass of pages was simply chewed to bits. It was impossible to piece together any coherent story. Only a word here and there gave us a clue to what had happened—the death of King Edward VII, a visit to France in an extra-prosperous year, apparently in the attempt to trace Monsieur's wife so that a divorce could be arranged which would enable him to marry Skivvy, who, although she never considered she was doing wrong in becoming Monsieur's mistress, seems always to have had a hankering to be made 'respectable.' The search was unsuccessful, but from what we could decipher Skivvy seems to have enjoyed her trip and to have been suitably shocked by the goings-on of some of the 'foreigners.' How disappointed Eve and I were at missing her graphic account of what she really thought of them!

A few pages which were only half-eaten enabled us to keep track of the main events in her story. Her Birdie survived the 1914–1918 War, with the loss of a leg and the acquisition of a D.S.O. 'At least if he'd lost one of his precious legs, he was out of the fighting line, and for that I thanked God many times on my knees,' writes Skivvy. When the next readable section came, the First World War was over, and Skivvy's Monsieur on the verge of achieving fame.

CHAPTER THIRTEEN

THE PRICE OF FREEDOM

THE FIRST really exciting piece of news I had when the War ended was that of my Birdie's marriage. It was my friend Letitia who brought it to me. She had read the announcement in *The Times* one day when she was tidying away her lady's papers, and she cut it out and kept it for me. He was marrying Lady Catherine, the daughter of the Duke of Learmouth, and it was to be the wedding of the year, at St. Margaret's, Westminster. I went to see it—I couldn't keep away, though I knew I was a fool to go. It would only wring my heart again to see him. But I went, and got there early, and managed to get a place close to the great stone entrance, and though I could scarcely see a thing because of the tears that clouded my eyes, I was glad I went.

My lady was there, leaning on my lord's arm. My lord, I thought, looked a very sick man, and, indeed, he died a year later. My lady's bright hair was threaded with grey and she was stouter than she used to be. But she was still beautiful and stately, wearing a dress of amethyst brocade, and carrying a bouquet of lovely flowers. The six bridesmaids wore pink organdy frocks and wreaths of roses on their hair, and the bride was in a wonderful dress of tulle and lace—and pretty she was, I must say, with crisp, curling auburn hair under her veil and bright, dark eyes.

But it was my Birdie I'd come to see, and as he came out of the church with his bride on his arm, he halted just on a level with me for the photographers to take them. I could almost have touched him if I'd reached out my arm. Oh, he was splendid to look at, my boy! A handsome, well-grown young man, broad-shouldered and brown-faced, with a bright smile and his blue eyes dancing with happiness. He'd learnt to manage his artificial leg so well that you could never have told there was a thing wrong when he walked. I'd heard that he could even dance with it. He looked so wonderful, and I felt so proud of him as he stood there that I couldn't help piping out 'Good luck and God bless you, sir'—I remembered to add the 'sir,' or it would have sounded cheeky. And he glanced round and smiled at me.

Whether he recognized me and knew that it was me who called out, I don't know. But he'd heard it anyway, and I was content—and then the photographers fell back and the bride and bridegroom passed on, and for me the day was over.

So the War ended, and life began again for us all. Monsieur got a regular job on a magazine drawing cartoons. I hadn't known he could do that sort of thing, but one day in a café, he was idly sketching just to amuse himself and a man at the next table saw them and was very impressed. He turned out to be the Features Editor of a big magazine, and he offered Monsieur a regular salary to do a weekly cartoon for him, which was a godsend. We rejoiced at this windfall, and began to make plans to move into a better studio flat, but the luck was too good to last. The greatest tragedy of my life was to come upon me, and it wasn't long in coming.

It was November again, just a year since the Armistice, and it was a very foggy month. There was a very bad fog one night when Monsieur went to visit his beloved club, *The Cercle Francais*. Looking out from the window of our top floor eyrie, I didn't like the look of it, and I begged him not to go, but he insisted. It was, he said, a special night. There was a celebration for somebody's birthday, and also he wanted to discuss with his friends the sending in of my picture, *After The Bath*, and one or two others he had painted, to the yearly exhibition at the Royal Academy. He said it was only a thickish mist, and was probably all right on the street level, and off he went whistling—and that was the last time I saw him alive.

He never came home that night. The fog thickened and visibility was only a foot or two beyond one's nose, so it would have been utterly useless for me to go out to look for him. When at last dawn began to break, I was still awake on the divan bed I had so often and so happily shared with my little man, so I got up and as soon as I thought it would be open, I groped my way to the chemist's shop at the corner, to ask if I might use the telephone. Although *The Cercle Francais* did not open till noon, I guessed that there would still be some of the members there who had had to stay the night because of the fog. And I was right. One of Monsieur's greatest friends spoke to me and was very concerned when he heard that Monsieur had not come home. He had left the club a little after midnight, though some of the members had tried to persuade him to stay until the fog had lifted a little. But he would not. His Emmee would worry, he said, and that he would not have for worlds.

So, in his care and love for me, he set forth, and met death on his groping way home. His body was found, the neck broken, at the bottom of a deep excavation in the street where men had been digging to repair a broken drain-pipe. The red lamps left by the workmen to give warning had been taken away—probably by some heedless young fools after a drunken party. And in the dark and fog he had fallen into it.

So he died—at the height of his power, with fame and success only a little way ahead of him. His body was brought home to me that morning when the fog lifted. And the dark clouds descended upon me—never really to pass again.

*   *   *

I am not going to even try to put down in writing what the loss of my darling Monsieur meant to me. I still can't bear to think of those awful months that followed his death, when I felt as though the bottom of my world had dropped out and I was left suspended in a sort of void, dazed and helpless, not knowing what to do or where to turn, and, worst of all, not caring.

There was quite a lot of stuff about

Monsieur in the papers, for some of his artist friends rallied round me and sent some of his pictures to an Exhibition where they attracted a good deal of attention and one or two of them were sold. Later a dealer came and bought up all the rest of them, and though he didn't pay me anything like what he must eventually have made from them, there was quite a nice sum to pay into my Post Office Savings account. Monsieur had made a will leaving everything to me, describing me as his 'Beloved friend and companion, Mrs. Emily Bligh,' so everything coming in from the sale of his pictures was mine. So thanks to that, and his foresight in making me put everything we could save into the Savings Bank, I really had quite a good nest-egg—enough to keep me from having to go out to work for my living until I had got over the shock and misery of my bereavement.

That was a miserable time, when night after night I lay alone crying in the darkness without even old Towser to keep me company. The poor old dog had been ailing for a long while, and soon after Monsieur's death he became so ill I had to get a vet to him. The vet said that he couldn't get well and it wasn't kind to let him go on suffering. So he gave me some pills with laudanum or something of that sort in them, and the dear old dog died quietly in his sleep without pain.

*   *   *

Now I am coming to a part of my story that I suppose I should be ashamed of, though I can't truthfully say that I am. It was, I think, eight or nine months after Monsieur's death that a knock came at the studio door—the landlord had allowed me to keep it on—about five o'clock in the afternoon. I opened the door, wondering who it could be—and there stood Tilda!

I was so astonished that I just stood and gaped at her for a minute. Tilda! And a Tilda changed very much for the worse since I had seen her at the White City Exhibition—she looked at least ten years older, even under the powder and paint. As I stood staring, she grinned at me and came mincing into the room on her high-heeled shoes.

'Well! Well! Don't look as if you've seen a ghost! I'm real enough, Skivvy. Your old crony Tilda in the flesh!'

She flopped into an armchair, and without even asking if she might, lit a cigarette. I pulled myself together, and shut the door, and then went over to her, making the usual sort of remarks one does make when one is startled and disconcerted. Tilda interrupted them.

'You needn't say you're glad to see me, for I can see very well you're not,' she said with a wry grin. 'But I told you at the White City that I should come along and see you one day, and here I am. S'matter of fact, I came along very soon after, but your old man barred the way like the blooming angel at the gate of the Garden of Eden. Didn't he ever tell you he'd met me coming up your stairs?'

'No, he didn't,' I said. I glanced at the stove. The kettle had begun to sing, and when it was boiling I supposed I'd have to offer Tilda a cup of tea, though I didn't want to. Tilda followed my gaze to the kettle.

'If you're thinking of tea you can count me out,' she told me bluntly. 'I won't say no, though, if you've got a drop of something stronger. Gin for preference.'

'I can give you a glass of wine,' I said. 'I'm afraid I haven't anything stronger. But you'd be wiser drinking tea, Tilda. It's only just after five o'clock, early to start drinking.'

'T'aint for me,' said Tilda. 'I'm just out of bed—I'm a night worker, you know—and I need something to pep me up a bit before I start out on my beat. It's changed now. I'm pounding the pavement now in the Edgeware

Road. Bit lower down in the social scale, but there's a good livin' to be made there.'

I had risen to get the wine and glass, but this flippant way of talking of the life she was leading I really couldn't stand.

'Look here, Tilda! I don't want to hear any details of your life. I'm just not interested. I don't want to be priggish, but your way of living isn't mine, and we haven't anything in common now that I can see. I can't think why you've come here like this.'

There was a pause, and Tilda drank a draught of the wine I'd poured out for her before she answered. Her sharp brown eyes looked at me with a gleam of malicious amusement over the rim of the glass, then, as she set the glass down, she said in a soft but meaningful tone:

'Nothing in common? Oh, come off it, Skivvy! *I* can think of something we have in common—something important! A certain adventure we had together long ago.'

I flushed. I knew very well what she meant.

'That's all past and done with, years ago,' I said. 'I'm not going to talk about it. Tell me, what did my husband say to you when you called, as you say you did?'

Tilda smiled an evil smile.

'Oh, he was very high and mighty! I ran

into him at the bottom of your stairs and asked him if Madam Yvetôt still lived here. I never guessed he was your husband or I wouldn't have spoken to him—I wanted a nice quiet chat alone with my old girl friend. I'd have thought you could have picked up somebody younger and better-looking than *him*, Skivvy.'

'Shut up about him,' I said angrily. 'How did you find my address, anyway? I never gave it to you.'

Tilda extracted a crumpled envelope from the depths of the ornate reticule she carried, and handed it to me. It was addressed to Lord Stilwell, and on it was my address, scribbled in my own handwriting. I remembered then my lord's handing me an old envelope to write my name and address on at the Exhibition, but I thought I had seen him put it into his pocket when I gave it him back. Tilda answered the question on my lips before I could frame it.

'I was listening, though you never saw me, and I saw that His Nibs hadn't put it properly into his pocket, there was a corner sticking out. I guessed that you'd never give your address to me, but I thought the time might come when I'd want to see you—so I pinched it out of his pocket in the crush. Got any more of that wine? It's not half bad.'

In stunned silence I poured her out another drink, and she went on:

'Well, I'll come to the point. I read in the papers about your man dying, and about the pictures he painted. They said how clever he was, and that people who bought his stuff to-day would probably find they'd made a good investment later on. So it was plain you were in the money. And I thought that, since there was no-one now to bar the way, I might as well drift along and see if you couldn't spare a pound or two for me.'

I was so astonished that for a moment or two I could only stare at her, while Tilda leant back in the arm-chair and eyed me mockingly, still smoking her cigarette.

'*Tilda!*' I exploded at last. 'What on earth do you mean? Why should I give you money—even if I'd got a lot to give, which I haven't.'

'You've got more than I have, anyway,' snapped Tilda. 'Look here, Skiv, I'm in damned low water. When your old man gave me the frozen mitt I decided that it didn't matter, for I was making good money then, and didn't really need any more. But I never could save a bean, and things aren't as good as they were, and also I'm getting older. Result is, I'm not getting the men I used to get, and I'm having to cut the price for those I *do* pick up. Used to get three pounds a go, easy—now I'm lucky if I get ten bob.'

I shuddered at the practical, everyday way in which she spoke of the price she asked for the sale of her body, and I said confusedly:

'I'm sorry, Tilda, but I still don't see what all this has got to do with me.'

'This is what. I want five quid. In fact, I've got to have it, to pay the rent of my bloody little attic in Praed Street. The old trout who runs the house is clamouring for it—it's already overdue more than two weeks. If I don't cough up by tomorrow I shall be out on my ear with no place to take a man to when I've caught one.'

Five pounds! It was more than two weeks of my living expenses, but I thought I could afford it—just once. I rose slowly to my feet and going into my little curtained bedplace I extracted five one-pound notes from my bag and returned with them in my hand.

'I'll give it to you this once,' I said. 'I can just manage it, and you can have it because I'm sorry for you and we used once to be friends. But it's no good your counting on it happening again. I used up most of the money

I got from the sale of Monsieur's pictures on paying for the funeral, and I'm working for my living now, as I used to do before I got married. I shan't be able to afford to give you any more.'

Tilda glanced round the studio, and her look was eloquent. 'Poor?' it said, 'With all these possessions around you, good clothes on your back, and a permanent home!' And, indeed, the studio was a very different place from what it was when I had first seen it. The walls had been redecorated, there was a good carpet on the floor and curtains at the windows to tone with it, a handsome patchwork quilt on the divan, and a set of pewter dishes which I'd polished like mad until they shone like silver. And there were other oddments here and there which we had picked up at various times. I knew without the need of words what Tilda's thoughts would be when she returned to her miserable, poky little room, which I could visualize well enough even though I had never seen it—and a wave of sorrowful pity came over me. On an impulse, I ran back to my purse and took out another pound which I pushed into Tilda's hand.

'There! It's more than I can manage, really, but I am sorry for you, Tilda, so very sorry.'

Well, I was trapped, as one so often is trapped by a sentimental sense of pity. Tilda thanked me and kissed me and departed, and I told myself ruefully that I had been a fool, but that, after all, she *had* helped me once, and that, anyway, it was unlikely I should ever see her again.

But in this I reckoned without Tilda! I suppose I was a fool not to realize that once she had made a successful kill, so to speak, she would come back for more. And I should have guessed from the hint she let drop about the secret that we shared in common, that this was really intended for a threat. But neither of these things crossed my mind then, and though I thought about Tilda a good deal after her visit, it was with pity that the pert, bonny little maid who had once been so good a friend to me, should be reduced to such a wreck, with her lined face and sunken eyes—not with any dread of her future intentions.

It was about a couple of months before she turned up again, and my face, as she walked into the studio must have been anything but welcoming, while my heart sank at the sight of her. She sank into a chair and threw her hat on to the table, revealing a shingle-cropped head of hair dyed a fierce chestnut colour.

'How d'you like my new hair-do, Skiv?' she asked. 'I thought my clients were getting a bit too used to the old Tilda, so I decided to spring a new one on 'em. Very successful it is, too.'

'If you *want* to know, I don't like it at all,' I told her. 'But I suppose that doesn't matter. But, look here, Tilda. I can't have you coming visiting me here—it doesn't look well.'

Tilda gave a snort of contemptuous laughter.

'Doesn't look well—deah me! Hark at Lady Clara Vere de Vere!' Then her jeering turned to sudden ferocity. 'Who the hell do you think you are, Skivvy, to talk like that? For all you've turned respectable, you've got a nasty patch in your past, you know, if it ever came out.'

I made no reply, fighting hard to keep my temper, and she went on:

'At least I haven't got a bastard kid foisted on to other people.'

That was more than I could stand. I caught Tilda a sound slap across the cheek. It rang through the quiet room, and for a full minute we stood glaring at each other—Tilda with her hand to her cheek, and I with my palm tingling and my heart thumping with mingled anger and fear. Yes, with fear—for the hard brown eyes boring into mine were as venomous now as the eyes of an angry snake.

Then at last Tilda spoke, and her voice was harsh with menace.

'You'll pay for that—and pay through the nose! You'll give me another fiver now, Skivvy—no, we'll make it ten while we're about it! You don't want me to visit you? Right—I won't come as long as you pay me to keep away. This time, it'll cost you ten quid. Fork it out—and I'll be off.'

'Ten quid! I can't!' I cried. 'Do you mean you're going to try and get money out of me every time you come?'

Tilda nodded.

'That's exactly what I do mean. Every time I come, you'll shell out something—and the longer you keep me waiting for it the more it's going to be.'

'But I *can't*!' I cried desperately. 'Honestly, Tilda, I haven't a lot put by. I could only just manage to give you that six pounds the other day.'

'Then you'll have to manage better for the future, for from now on, you'll have to count me in. What a fool you are, Skivvy, not to see you're trapped. You've *got* to play ball with me—or somebody you care for more than anyone else in the world is going to suffer.'

I gasped and stared at her speechless, and she went on:

'Still all at sea? Well, if I've got to put it into words of one syllable, here it is. You'll shell out for me when I ask you, Skiv, or I'll go down to the Manor House and spill the beans about your damn Birdie. They'll believe me—they'll have to. Think I've forgotten where we buried it? You can bet they'll pay me whatever I ask to hold my tongue. So, if you don't want 'em to be bothered, Skivvy, you'll have to do the paying.'

I was too stunned with horror to say anything. But I knew I was beaten. My darling's whole life was in danger, and there was nothing I could do to save him but obey. I went and got the money Tilda demanded and gave it to her, and she went—and from that time onwards I never knew a moment's peace until—but I will come to that soon.

*   *   *

Sometimes she would turn up every week, sometimes she'd leave me alone for a month, depending upon the number of lovers she found and how generous they were. Sometimes, when she was in a good mood, she

250

would ask for only two or three pounds—at other times she would be as hard as nails and demand as much as she thought I had by me. After a few months the drain on my precious nest-egg became so marked that I grew panic-stricken, and my fear and anger grew into a dull, steady hate that sometimes frightened me. I found a job cooking in a little restaurant and I wore myself out by day trying to do more and more work to make up my losses, and by night I lay awake, trying to think of some way out of the desperate *impasse* I was in. The prospect of finding myself penni-less—as I was bound to do sooner or later if this drain on my slender earnings went on—and then have Tilda carry her demands for payment for her silence to Birdie or my lady, as I felt certain she would do, sent me almost demented.

Probably she would go to my lady, as the person most likely to bribe her to keep silence. Kind-hearted as Lady Stilwell was, she would never refuse to grant an interview to anyone who had once been in her service, and I knew that Tilda would be too clever to present her-self at the Manor as the painted trollop she was now. Oh, no! She would abjure make-up and wear the soberest clothes she possessed and appear in the character of a humble working-woman who could bear the burden of a guilty secret no longer. Yes, the interview would start like that. Tilda was a good actress, as I had reason to know. Only too vividly I could picture the growing bewilderment and fear, and finally the stricken look on my lady's face as her dream was shattered before her eyes—the dream that had kept her proud and happy for years. Her boy, her adored Freddie, shown to be no child of hers, but a changeling foisted upon her—the son of a butler and of little Emily Bligh, once her tweeny-maid! The vision was too agonizing, and I writhed and wept in anguish as I saw it enacted in dreadful clarity in my mind's eye night after night as I lay sleepless in my crumpled bed. And day by day, I saw the dark cloud growing nearer the final crash when Tilda would have milked me of every penny I possessed and would turn her attention to my dear lady. She would get what she wanted from her, I was sure. Whatever it cost her to realize that the child she adored was not, after all, flesh of her flesh and bone of her bone, my lady would pay—pay and pay again to keep the knowledge from Birdie and his aristocratic young wife.

I prayed and prayed to be shown some way out. I went to church more often than I had ever done since my childhood, and when I didn't get any answer to my prayers in the church I had been brought up in, I went to Monsieur's little Roman church, and for a little while I found a sort of forlorn comfort in the glowing colours, the smell of the incense, the soft music, and the many candles, like tiny crocus flowers clustering around the feet of the statues of the saints. But nothing happened to lighten for long the weight of hate and fear that lay so heavily upon me—until, suddenly, a way out was shown to me.

But it wasn't shown to me by God. It was shown to me by the Devil.

*   *   *

It was dark and foggy that evening when Tilda came to see me. It was late, and I wasn't expecting her, for she generally called in the afternoon before she set out on her ignoble 'beat.' Outside the snow was falling, and Tilda came in shivering, in spite of her leopard-skin coat and cap, and her high-heeled Russian boots—Russian boots were all the rage just then. A dull, burning anger rose within me. Christmas was only a few weeks ahead, and the few pounds I had managed to save for it were now to be taken from me. But

253

I dared not show the fury that raged within me. I masked it with a false smile of welcome and went to get the wine she always demanded, while she threw open her coat and warmed her hands at the fire.

'Lucky you,' she said sourly, to be able to sit here in comfort while I've got to walk the damn streets touting for customers.'

'Well, you needn't,' I said brusquely as I poured out the wine. 'You're good at dressmaking, and I could get you several customers at once if you'd only chuck what you're doing now and make a fresh start. There's a lady in the flat downstairs wants someone to make some clothes for her. I'm doing a bit of knitting for her, and she asked me only the other day didn't I know a dressmaker I could recommend.'

'We've been over that before,' said Tilda tartly. 'And I've told you the answer. You don't catch me sitting on my backside stitching for bitches. Oh, I'm not doing so badly! I get 'em still, though not as quickly and easy as I used to. And anyhow'—she looked at me with a malicious little smile—'I've got you to fall back upon if I strike a bad patch.'

'Well, there's one thing I'm looking forward to,' I said, bitterly. 'When you have squeezed everything I possess out of me, I shan't see you again.'

'Don't you be too sure of that,' said Tilda. 'You might see your way, a little later on, to come in with me, Skiv. Oh, don't pop your eyes at me! I mean it. A couple of girls working a street together, turn and turn about, often do damn well. You've worn well enough to pass for ten years younger than you are—and that figure of yours always drew the men.'

I found my voice at last. I had been so furious at Tilda's blazing effrontery that I had been quite speechless at first. What I said was blasting, but Tilda only grinned that malicious grin of hers.

'Don't be too sure you won't come to it,' she commented. 'After all, there is your Birdie to consider, you know!' She rose to her feet as she spoke and looked at the window. Snow was falling steadily, and a thick white line was beginning to pile up aganst the glass.

'Oh, hell!' she said. 'And I've got to go out in it. If you'll come across with a quid or two, Skivvy—let's say four, ain't that nice of me to be so reasonable to-night? If you'll let me have four I've a mind to go back and have a night in bed all to myself for once.'

She looked at me, as, with my jaw set, I went on knitting and made no effort to move.

Then her tone suddenly became menacing.

'Come on, Skiv, hand it over! And if you've got any more of those headache tablets you gave me once, the ones you say your Monsieur used when he had a headache, you can give me one of those as well. I've got a regular splitter coming on—another reason why I want a virtuous night.'

I rose reluctantly to my feet. It was no use protesting—she wouldn't go until she'd got what she had come for. But as I walked towards the screened off part of the room where I kept my personal belongings, my heart was murderous within me. They say that when one reaches a certain pitch of rage one sees red—and it's true! By the time I reached my chest-of-drawers everything seemed to be swirling round me in a mist of red—a dreadful, lurid, murky red.

I took the money from the box in which I had put it, and rummaged in the drawer for the round white box of headache tablets which Tilda wanted. I found them—and beside them I saw another box, the box that had held the poison tablets the vet had given me for Towser. I touched it and the lid fell off, and two tablets lay revealed. Round white tablets, practically the same size and shape as the tablets in the other box. It seemed that I stood staring at them for a long time, transfixed, unable to move. But really, I suppose it was only a matter of seconds, and then—and then I found myself walking back to Tilda, who was pouring herself another glass of wine, and I was holding out the notes in one hand, and in the other the box marked '*Cachets Faivre*.'

'Here you are,' I said, and it astonished me that my voice sounded just as normal as usual. 'Here's the money, and here—'

I all but faltered, but Tilda was paying no attention to me. She pounced on the money and the box, stuffed the notes into her bag and then, taking both the tablets, popped them into her mouth and washed them down with a long draught of wine.

'There!' she said, as she put the wine-glass down. 'I've taken 'em both to be on the safe side. Now I'll be off to seek my downy. Bobs your uncle, Skiv, and if you can't be good, be careful!'

The door shut behind her, and I heard the click of her heels descending the steep, uncarpeted stairs. It was done! I had committed murder. And I wasn't sorry! I'm not sorry even now, all these years after. It was Tilda or my Birdie—his life, his future, his happiness. I'm an old woman now and it can't be long before I have to meet my Maker—yet, if I was faced to-day with the same situation, I'd do it all over again!

Oh, I'm not going to say it didn't affect me! It *did*. When I began to be able to move again after she'd gone, I found myself in a cold sweat. And then I started to shake like a jelly and wanted to cry—and then began to laugh wildly at myself for wanting to. For why should I cry when Birdie and I were safe at last? I heated up some coffee to get myself warm again and took some brandy as well—and then I started picturing Tilda walking back to Praed Street through the falling snow. The murderous tablets that had given old Towser his merciful release would be working stealthily within her. As I swallowed my coffee and huddled, shivering, over the fire, I wondered how long in the case of a human being those tablets would take to act. It was impossible to tell, but I hoped that Tilda would get back to her room before they became effective. I knew, from the effect they had had on Towser, that at first she would just feel sleepy. Then the sleep that came upon her would gently merge into the sleep of death. She would die without pain—the vet had assured me of that when he gave me the tablets for Towser. As the night went on, I hoped desperately that she would reach the place she called home in time. The thought of her falling down and dying in the snow-filled street worried me and I wondered vaguely why, when I had found the strength to put into her hands the poison that would kill her, I should bother now as to how and where death overtook her. Yet somehow I did.

I sat there, crouched over the fire almost until dawn, picturing with agonizing vividness what might be happening to the woman I had deliberately sent to her death. Oddly enough, the danger to myself, the possibility that inquiries might be made, her visit to the studio become known and the tablets traced to me, never struck me. It was only Tilda I thought about, and when at last, exhausted with shock and strain, I fell asleep in the armchair, it was to dream about the early days at the Manor when Tilda and I were friends, before the coming of Valentine changed the course of my life.

When I awoke in the morning, I could scarcely believe that the events of the previous evening hadn't all been part of the dream. Was it possible that I, Emily Bligh, had deliberately and of set intention murdered a fellow human being? Well, it was done—and even had I wanted to draw back now, it was too late. For good or ill the thing must have happened by this time. Unless—and at the thought my heart leaped with fear—unless the poison in the tablets had lost its strength. It was some time since I had put Towser to sleep and it was possible—just possible—that. the drug had grown weaker by keeping. Possibly Tilda had merely been very sick and was still alive! This thought drove me nearly silly for many hours—then my mind was set at rest by a remark from Madame Franz, the lady in the downstair flat, when I went that evening to deliver the knitting she had ordered from me. Having admired the knitting I had done and paid me, Madame Franz, a pleasant Belgian woman who had come to England as a refugee in the war and had remained in London with her family, said, as she nodded towards the ' window outside which the snow was still driving:

'A terrible night again, Madame Yvetôt! One is thankful to be indoors. Those poor ones who have no home, how one's heart bleeds for them! Did you hear of the terrible discovery made this morning, only just a few streets away from here? A woman found dead in the snow?'

My heart seemed to stop beating, but I heard myself say quite normally.

'No! How dreadful. Who was it? Anyone we know?'

'Oh, no! Only a *grue*, a street-walker, not known in this neighbourhood. These poor ones, they have few friends. When they die it is little more than the passing of a stray dog or cat. May our Lady have mercy on her soul!'

It was true. When I left Madame Franz I went out and bought an evening paper and read about it in that. Tilda had evidently got some distance before the sleepiness induced by the tablets had come upon her, and then it seemed she had taken refuge in the doorway of a block of offices, where some steps led up to a deep porch. Here she would be sheltered from the snow and could rest for a few minutes—and there she was found by the care-taker who came to open up the offices in the morning. It was thought at first that she had died from the cold. But there was an inquest, and it was found that her death was due to some form of laudanum poisoning. Nobody could discover, though, where she had got the laudanum or why she had taken it. She had money in her bag, and was well-dressed for a street-walker, and had a room in Praed Street, the rent of which had been paid up to date. Oh, yes, they traced her as far as that—but they got no further. And after the inquest was over, with its verdict of suicide, the story dropped out of the papers, as Tilda dropped out of my life.

It was over. I was free, and—what was far more important—Birdie was safe. Even though it has cost me my immortal soul—and it may well have done, I know—I had saved him and I did not regret it. I had done a hideous thing, but it was worth doing.

CHAPTER FOURTEEN

AT THE WARDEN'S POST

I GAVE up writing for a long time after I left the studio that had been my happy home with my darling little Monsieur, and I never really thought that I should take it up again. I had to leave, for Tilda had taken all my little nest-egg, and the money I was earning wasn't enough to pay the rent and keep me beside. So I found a room nearer where I was working, which was much cheaper. It was very small, but it was unfurnished so that I was able to have some of my things around me; and the rest Papa Condé, of the *Cercle Francais*, the club Monsieur had belonged to, offered to store for me free of charge in the cellar—a tribute to Monsieur's memory, he said.

It was because of Monsieur that I never threw away the mountain of manuscript I found I had collected, when I was sorting things out in the studio, preparatory to leaving it. 'Always finish a job if you've begun it,' was one of his favourite sayings. I hesitated when I came across the pile and saw how big it had become. Should I burn it, and with it the memories of my early years? I wouldn't have space to store much in my one small room. But no! I decided I wouldn't burn it. He had wanted it begun, he had read much of it, approved it and revised it. In many places there were corrections in his writing. It was too intimately connected with him for me to bear to destroy it. Some day, when I felt like it, maybe I would go on with it, I told myself.

So I dumped the whole pile of papers into the bottom of a trunk with a lot of other little treasures, and sent the trunk round to Papa Condé, and for many years I almost forgot about it. But when I came here, to the Dower House, to settle down at last, and was given this lovely room to use as my own 'for the rest of your life' they said, I sent for the trunk. The *Cercle Francais* had somehow managed to escape the bombs of the Second World War which had laid flat so much of Soho, and my trunk was intact. I got those who waited on me to set out my little treasures, the things that mattered so much to me, things that had belonged to my life with Monsieur—the only part of my life when I had been truly happy. Though a little of that happiness came back when I looked round this pretty room and saw on the mantel-piece and on the shelves which they had cleared for me, the treasures I hadn't seen for so many years—the photograph of Monsieur, the pewter dishes, the majolica plates we'd picked up in Italy, a cuckoo clock and all the rest. There was room for them all and to spare, and when they were all in place I couldn't help but cry, I was so happy to be surrounded with them all again.

And after awhile, since except for a bit of knitting, I've nothing else to do, I've decided I'd try to round off this story before I died, the story of my unimportant life. But I haven't the energy to write down everything that happened to me after the death of Tilda and my leaving the studio. It would take too long and my memory isn't what it was, either. I'm seventy now, so it isn't surprising, I think, that I can't recall things as well as a younger woman might have done. I shall just put down what I remember best and leave it at that. If I miss out bits or put them in the wrong order, it won't matter. After all, I'm only going to finish this because of Monsieur, and because I hope that when I die I'll see him again, and hear him say, 'Well done, Emmee! Always finish what you've begun.'

Well, after the Tilda business I wasn't sorry to leave the studio. I wasn't sorry I'd killed her, not a bit—though the thought of the way she'd died, alone in the cold in the street, did worry me rather. I felt angry with God that He couldn't have answered my prayer and let her keep awake until she'd reached her own bed. I wouldn't have minded half so much her dying there. But after awhile the whole thing faded out, and if anybody tells me that murderers are haunted by their crimes, I can tell 'em it's rubbish. They aren't. They forget about them in time—as I practically forgot about Tilda. Once, when my friend Letitia asked me if I'd ever seen her again, it did give me a bit of a start. But I answered in a flash: 'Oh, dear me, no!' And that was that. I hardly ever thought about it afterwards.

I'd had enough of cooking at the little restaurant, and decided to go back to domestic service, as I thought it offered an easier life as well as a better-paid one. But I was quite determined that I wouldn't live in again. I'd grown too used to my freedom at nights to give it up. After all, I was forty-five—not a girl any more—and I needed to be quiet and alone after my working-day was done. I wondered whether my determination not to sleep in would make it difficult for me to find a job, but Letitia, with whom I discussed my plans, said no, not any longer. Things had changed a lot since the war, and servants weren't so easy to get and wanted more liberty as well as more money. Quite a lot of girls now had daytime jobs. Letitia was very kind, and it was she who found me my first post—and who do you think it was with? Miss Sybil of all people!

Mrs. Fortescue had died during the war, and Mr. Fortescue had married again. And soon after Miss Sybil had married, too, and had a fine house in Egerton Square. Letitia had gone to work for her, and she knew that she wanted someone else, someone who could cook. I thought that perhaps she wouldn't want me after what happened when I left her mother's service. But Letitia said that she wouldn't mind that. In fact, she said, Miss Sybil had stuck up for me about that, for her brother had told her the truth, and she was sure I'd be taken on if I applied. So I did, and Miss Sybil was delighted, and I stayed with her for five or six years and could have stayed longer if I'd been willing to go down into the country and sleep in. There was a baby by this time, and Miss Sybil and her husband thought it would be better for it to grow up in country air. Letitia agreed to go with them, but I felt I was out of tune for the country now, and all my friends were in London, for I'd kept up with most of those who used to come and see Monsieur. So I stayed in London and found another job, though just what it was I'm not sure now. It's funny how, as one grows older, one remembers some things so very clearly, while others get dim or else fade out. I suppose it's only the things that really matter that stand out when one's getting old. The lesser ones die. After Monsieur died and I'd got rid of Tilda, the only really important thing in my life was my son, and what I could learn about him. My lady, too, I could never forget, though there were times when I wondered whether I loved her or hated her. Perhaps I did both—for indeed I couldn't help loving her for her gentleness and kindness, and yet I hated her for having what I ought to have had—the long years with my child. She had watched him grow from babyhood into a boy, and then into splendid young manhood—and though I had given her this gift myself, that did nothing to prevent my resenting her having it. But I grieved deeply when I heard that she had died quietly in her sleep one night, shortly after the birth of my Birdie's son. She and my lord had been devoted to one another, and after he had died and she had seen his son and heir—queer how it hurts me still to write that lie!—happily married, she had nothing more to live for and just faded out.

I remember that I worked for a time in a

sort of Remand Home for girls that had got into trouble, but I soon had enough of that. After a mutiny when they went rampaging through the place breaking windows and crockery and setting fire to curtains, I gave in my notice, for I felt I was getting too old to stand that kind of life. And I had a job with a scientific old gentleman, whose house was packed with curious things he had brought back from his travels. One of them was an Egyptian mummy that stood upright in a corner of his sitting-room and gave me quite a turn when I first saw it. I stayed with him a long while, but then he went and got married and I just couldn't abide his wife. She couldn't abide me, either, and I overheard her telling the professor that it was absurd having a woman there all day, and it would be cheaper to get somebody in just for the mornings and go out for meals except for simple things she could cook herself. The professor seemed rather sorry.

'It's a pity,' he said. 'Mrs. Bligh's made me very comfortable all these years'—I'd taken to calling myself Mrs. Bligh again, for people pronounced 'Madame Yvetôt' in such odd ways that it irritated me, and anyway I'd never been married to Monsieur. 'And she's a first-class cook.'

So, seeing Madam meant to get rid of me, I got in first and told her I'd like to go. And after that I went from one job to another until at last I landed up with a dear old lady who lived in a tall, old-fashioned house in Montague Square, of which she'd let the upper half, and lived herself on the ground floor with her cat and her canary, her radio and her gramophone, and her old French maid. She had been a famous opera singer in her youth—Madame Maritza Pulaski—and her flat was crammed with treasures from her career. Eloise, her maid, told me that the cellars underneath the house were full of trunks and crates, packed with presents from kings and nobles—tea and dinner services in priceless china, toilet sets in solid gold, and carpets, and hangings and valuable furniture and heaven knows what else. And from the lovely things strewn carelessly about in the rooms Madame used, I could quite believe what Eloise said about the rest.

The old lady wanted a daily woman who could cook really well and do the housekeeping. Eloise did all the rest—and it turned out a very nice place. Madame didn't go out very often for she was crippled with arthritis, but she had lots of friends who came to see her, and then she would often put on some of her old records on the gramophone, and Eloise and I would hear the voice that had been world-famous twenty years earlier, ringing through the flat. It was a clear, high soprano, pure and sweet as a boy's and she took her high notes as clearly and lightly as a boy would do. She was a gay, merry old lady, and when she was dressed for a party, in gleaming satin with her white hair piled high on the top of her head and a black lace mantilla draped over it, and diamonds round her throat and on her ears and fingers, she was a sight worth seeing, I can tell you! She usually had friends in to supper and cards once a week, and my cooking was highly praised. She liked good food, did Madame, and so did Eloise. I got on well with Eloise directly she heard me speak French, and we became fast friends. And there I stayed and worked happily enough until, once more, war came to England.

★   ★   ★

Well, I thought the First World War had been as bad as anything could be. But it was nothing to what we Londoners had to go through in the Second one! Even now, though it's all been over a long time, I still dream of having to find my way home through the darkened streets with search-lights ranging the sky overhead and wardens and police on the lookout for any light bigger than a three-penny bit in one's torch—and that directed on the ground or there'd be trouble! I hear in my dreams that dreadful moaning wail of the air-raid warning that told us raiders were on their way, and we must take cover in the nearest shelter. But how was an old lady in her eighties and so lame she could hardly hobble a yard, to get in time to any air-raid shelter? The cellars under Madame's house were deep and big enough to make a fairly good shelter, and Madame had chairs and carpets taken down, and installed heaters and a radio, and told everyone in the house to take refuge there when the warning signal went. Which they did, those, at least who didn't leave London. Eloise used to go down, too, if the raids were really bad. She stuck it out upstairs with Madame and me as long as she could, running her rosary beads through her fingers and praying. But she was a nervy sort, and after a time she would get so shaky that Madame would order her to go down to the cellar.

Madame's friends tried to persuade her to leave London, but Madame wouldn't go. She wasn't going to be driven out of her home by a damned Austrian house-painter, she said disdainfully—she who had been fêted and feasted by kings! She was old and ready to die if her time had come, but move she would not. And she used to sit at her window in her darkened drawing-room watching through binoculars the progress of the enemy aircraft as they swept across the sky, or the glow from the fires that blazed up from stricken houses here and there.

With raid warnings coming every night, and the dark streets in the winter months, it wasn't safe, and sometimes not possible, to get from Montague Square to my home at night. So I agreed to sleep in at Madame's for the winter, anyway, and I used to make up a bed on the divan in the drawing-room and sleep there—that is, when it was possible to sleep at all. But I kept my little room in Soho on, all the same, and as it turned out it was lucky for me that I did so. For one day—or rather one evening—when I had my day off and went to see some friends of Monsieur's, there was an especially heavy raid, and they wouldn't let me try to go back until the All Clear went, which it didn't do for a long time. When at last it did go and I made my way home—by Tube, I remember that night, instead of by bus as I did usually—and reached the corner of the road leading into Montague Square, I was pulled up short by a crowd milling about and policemen moving them on. And when at length I managed to push through the people and turned the corner—mercy on us! Madame's house just wasn't there! A bomb had dropped close behind it, and the whole group of buildings had been blasted to ruin— just a ghastly mountain of broken bricks and mortar.

The police wouldn't let me get near, though I told them I was Madame's cook. The house had collapsed like a thing built of cards, and there wasn't any hope that anyone could be alive underneath it. My poor old Madame was dead, and her faithful Eloise with her— and all I could do was to hope that death had come so quickly for both of them, that neither of them had known anything about it and hadn't suffered.

There were rescuers working madly on the ruins while the police held back the crowd. The family in the first floor flat had gone to the country long ago, and the only two people in the house beside Madame and Eloise, a young man and his wife, had taken refuge in the cellar in the only corner of it where the ceiling hadn't fallen, and they were dragged out alive with only minor injuries. But

Madame and Eloise were both dead, and as I saw their bodies brought out the tears ran down my face for thankfulness, for I was near enough to hear the doctor say that they must have been killed instantly and couldn't have suffered. I caught a glimpse of Madame's face as they lifted her on to a stretcher, and it was quite untouched, and, it seemed to me, her lips were curved in a faintly mocking smile, as though she were saying to Hitler—'You have killed my body, but you can't kill my spirit— it defies you even in death.' She was a dauntless old lady, my old Madame. May God rest her soul!

As she was carried away, a tall man who had been directing the rescue operations, paused for a moment close beside me. He was issuing orders to the men, and there was something about his voice which made me turn and stare up at him. He was grimy to a degree, having been working as hard as any of his men, but underneath all the grime I recognized him. It was my Birdie—and my heart seemed to leap into my throat and then start beating like a drum. How many years since I had seen him! And now I was growing into an old woman and he was no longer a young man—but to see him again, and in such circumstances! I had not even known he was in

London. I had imagined that he was down in the country, at the Manor House—for I knew that his artificial leg would have kept him out of the army in this war.

He moved away, and a policeman came up to me as I stood staring after him.

'Now, missus, move on,' the policeman said, kindly enough. 'You were the old girl's cook, you said, weren't you? Lucky for you that you were out when this happened.'

'Yes,' I said, still in a daze. 'But tell me, who was that? That tall gentleman who was standing here just now giving orders?'

'That?' said the policeman. 'Oh, that's Lord Stilwell. Air Raid Warden for the district, and a damn good chap, too, I can tell you. Got his team drilled like soldiers and works like the devil himself. Has a list of rescues as long as your arm to his credit.'

He moved on and I walked away—to think over what I had just heard and, if I could, to make use of it.

*   *   *

When I realized that at last—at last!—I was within hail of my son, my darling, my boy baby who had never, no matter what happened to me, lost his place in my heart, I set about planning my campaign as craftily as any general ever planned a battle. It was easy to find the Air Raid Warden's Post where Lord Stilwell was chief. It was in Marylebone, in a little street near Dorset Square. I discovered, in the course of my inquiries, that his wife, Lady Stilwell, was running a convalescent home for wounded soldiers at the Manor House, and his son, whom they had called Evelyn—a queer name, I thought, for a boy—was somewhere at school. My Birdie— he was always 'My Birdie' to me—was supposed to be living at his club when he was not on duty—though from what I could hear he was scarcely ever off duty; but he spent his days, and his nights, too, usually, at the Post, eating and sleeping when and as he could. I discovered, too, that these posts were mostly filled by men, for the work of digging people out of ruins and helping to put out fires was too heavy for women to do. So I figured that if a capable woman offered to come and help by keeping the offices clean and making tea for the workers, she might be very welcome. So one day I set out to seek my Birdie, praying that there weren't women volunteers enough at his Post.

I was thankful then as never before that I had always looked younger than I really was, for I knew that if I had appeared old and frail I wouldn't have had a chance of getting taken on. Though I was now well into my sixties, I was still upright and brisk in my movements, and my face, being round, hadn't fallen into the haggard lines that so often age an oval-shaped face. I put on my plainest coat and a small hat and brushed my greying hair out of sight beneath it, and felt sure that I could pass at most for a woman in her fifties. My heart was thumping when I walked into the Warden's headquarters, the ground floor of a dilapidated shop, two rooms and a basement, and I drew a breath of satisfaction when I saw how untidy and dusty the place was. It was obvious that no woman was working there. It was furnished with all sorts of oddments, plainly borrowed from anybody who had anything to spare, and in the main room there were two camp beds, heaped with army rugs and dirty pillows, gumboots crusted with mud, mackintoshes, rucksacks, spades and hatchets, a box of First Aid stuff, and heaven knows what beside.

I took all this in only vaguely that first day, because behind a desk littered with papers, a tall man was sitting—my Birdie! In the clear light of day, fantastic as it may sound, I could see in the face of the man of fifty, traces still of the baby I had adored. As he raised his head, my boy's own blue eyes looked at me, unchanged, clear, direct. For a moment I was so shaken that I couldn't speak. Then as he looked at me inquiringly, I pulled myself together and walked up to the desk.

'Good afternoon, sir. Am I speaking to Lord Stilwell, please?'

He nodded and surveyed me with keen but kindly eyes.

'Yes, that's right. Is there anything I can do for you?'

'It's rather what I can do for you, sir,' I said, steadily. 'I was cook to poor Madame Pulaski, who was killed when the bomb hit her house in Montague Square.'

'Ah, yes! Poor old Pulaski. Her cook, eh? But how did you—'

'It was my night out. I got back just after it happened, and saw you directing the digging—and—well, sir, now she's gone, poor lady, I'm out of a job, and I want—I'd like—' I was floundering a little now, for I couldn't very well tell him that my one desire was to be near him, to serve him, to help him, 'I'd like to know if you could use me here, sir? To clean and tidy the place, and maybe do a bit of cooking if you wanted any done.'

He looked up at a young man who had

come in and was standing at his side.

'What about it, David?' he asked. Then turning to me: 'I think we'd welcome any help you could give. But it's hard work, you know, and irregular, and if you have a family—'

'I haven't, sir,' I said. 'I'm alone in the world and if you'd let me come and work here I'd feel I was—was doing my bit towards winning the war. Please let me come, sir? I'm fit and strong and not afraid of work or long hours.'

'Well, we're certainly in need of someone to try and keep us in some sort of order,' he said. 'Right, Mrs.—by the way, what is your name?'

I don't quite know why it was. Maybe, it was seeing him that prompted it—brought back old memories, as it were. But before I knew it I'd said: 'Skeffington, sir, Mrs. Skeffington.'

He wrote it down carefully. 'And your address?'

I gave him the address of my room in Soho, and added that I was leaving there, as I'd had the chance of a room in Marylebone. That wasn't true, but I meant to make it true as soon as I could, and his face cleared.

'Oh, if you're coming to live somewhere handy, it will make a lot of difference,' he said. 'If you had to risk the journey back to Soho every night—well, that's fine. When can you start?'

But I was already taking off my coat and putting on the overall I'd brought with me in my bag.

'At once, sir, if you'll let me. This place needs cleaning—it's in a dreadful state.'

The two men looked at each other and laughed.

'That's what I call quick action!' said Birdie. 'You're right, Mrs. Skeffington—this place is a pigsty, but what else can you expect with a bunch of men? We had a good woman helping us till last week, but then her house was blitzed and she was hurt and had to be taken to hospital. We'll be more than obliged to you if you'll step in and take her place.'

And so my work at the Warden's Post began.

Luckily I knew some people in the district, and I didn't have much difficulty in finding a room to let. People were running away from London and there were plenty of vacant places. It was a dirty little room, and the woman who ran the house was always more or less drunk, but I didn't care. I meant to spend most of my time at the Post, and, anyway, I could keep my own room clean, whatever the rest of the place was like.

There were all sorts of people who came in and out of the Warden's Post, but the regulars were Birdie—The Chief, he was always called—Mr. David Crump, poor Mr. Benyon, who had T.B., and Mr. Loftus who was a poet. And besides them there was a languid young lady who wore trousers and a leather coat, who used to lounge in most days to share the typing work with a homely little body named Mrs. Anderson. The Honourable Miss Valerie Fitzroy rather scared me at first, but after awhile I realized that she meant to be friendly and pleasant, and I got quite to like her in the end. It was she who got out of me that I'd nursed Lord Stilwell when he was a baby, though I'd never meant to mention it.

It happened this way. Besides cleaning, I did any odd bits of mending or washing that was needed and I was always making tea or Bovril, or cooking a scrappy meal for someone who had been up all night. I tried my hardest to divide my attentions equally between everyone at the Post, and I'm certain sure I never refused to do anything for anybody. But they say, don't they? that love, money, and a cough, are three things that can never be hidden—and I suppose that when my Birdie asked me to do something for him, I did it just that much quicker and more eagerly without realizing it than I did for the others. Anyway, after awhile, Miss Fitzroy began to tease me about 'making a pet of the Chief,' it stung me into saying defensively that I didn't.

'Oh, yes you do!' said the young lady. 'He always gets the first cup of tea and the best bit of cake, and if he's tired when he comes in and goes to sleep, you stand by like a little watchdog and snarl if anyone makes a noise. I don't blame you—he's a grand man, and I've quite a soft corner for him myself.'

I said then what I'd never meant to let out, but I felt that some reason had to be given for my special interest in Lord Stilwell.

'Well, you see, miss, I've a special reason to want to look after my lord. I held him in my arms when he was a baby. When he was born I was a maid in his mother's house.'

'Were you, really?' Miss Fitzroy was quite thrilled. 'You were his nurse? Oh, well, no wonder you fuss over him. Does he know?'

I shook my head, and she went on:

'Oh, I must tell him! Oh, yes, I must, he'll be so interested. And, anyway, why should you want to keep it secret? Do tell me more? How long were you there and why did you leave?'

I wasn't prepared to detail the story of my life to her. But I said that I had worked at the Manor House for several years before Lady Stilwell's son had been born, and that, soon after his birth, I left to be married. I purposely left her under the impression that I had been his nurse, for though it wasn't strictly true, it gave me a better standing in the eyes of those who heard the story, and, after all, there was nobody left alive who could contradict me. I knew that Miss Fitzroy would pour out the tale to Lord Stilwell the first chance she got, and, sure enough the moment I arrived at the Warden's Post the next morning and found him talking to Mr. Crump, he turned and came across to me.

'Why, Mrs. Skeffington, what is this I hear? You are an old nurse of mine and you never told me!' He put his hand on my shoulder as he spoke, and my foolish heart swelled so high with sudden emotion that I had to hold on tight to my self-control as I replied in confusion that I hadn't quite liked to—that I felt rather shy—that I didn't know if he'd be interested. He cut me short when I said that.

'Of course, I'm interested! But you must have left when I was very much of a baby, for the Nanny I remember died at the Manor House when I was ten.'

'Oh, I wasn't the real Nanny, my lord,' I said hastily. 'I was only a young girl then, and wouldn't have been allowed the full responsibility of looking after you. But my lady, your mother, needed a lot of care after you were born, and your Nanny was often with her, so I was able to be with you a lot. You were still only a baby when I left to get married, so you wouldn't remember me, of course.'

'No, I suppose I wouldn't,' he said. 'Yet, it's odd, I thought there was something familiar about your face when you walked in here first. I felt as though I'd seen you somewhere, though I couldn't remember where.'

'You had, sir. Do you remember the Exhibition they called the White City.' I asked. 'That's where you saw me. I was there with a friend, and ran into my lord and lady, your father and mother, and they were kind enough to stand and talk to me for a few minutes. And you came up from a trip on the boats and shook my hand. I think you were about fifteen.'

'*Now* we're getting somewhere!' said my lord. 'I remember. I came up from my umpteenth trip on the lake and found you talking to my mother and father. I remember that, when we were driving home, my mother kept saying how pleased she was to see you again. She called you by some nick-name or other— what was it now? It stuck in my mind for quite a long time because it was so comic.'

I smiled.

'I know what it was, sir. It was "Skivvy"'

Miss Fitzroy, who had been listening to the conversation, gave a squeal of delight.

'Skivvy! Oh, what a gem of a name! Do you mind if we call you Skivvy? Skeffington is such a mouthful.'

'Of course I don't mind, miss,' I said. 'I've been Skivvy nearly all my life, and I've got quite to like the name.'

*   *   *

Apart from my years with Monsieur, the months that followed after that day were the happiest of my life, in spite of the fact that they were set against the hideous background of war. Day by day one lived in constant expectation of death. Seldom a week passed without some bad raid on London, and the news from the front grew steadily worse. And yet, because I was working alongside my son, sharing his danger and, I knew, lightening a little the burden he carried, I was happy— more than happy.

The place in which we worked was an old shop with a lot of glass about it. My lord had criss-cross strips of strong paper pasted over all the windows, so that, if they cracked, the glass wouldn't shoot about all over the place and hurt people. The cellar in the basement, too, had been cleared out, and the camp beds, and some old mattresses, and a few chairs, had been put in it, so that anybody who was able to snatch an hour or so of sleep, could have it in comparative safety. And when Miss Fitzroy brought in an oil stove and a carpet which she said she'd pinched from the house of an aunt who'd gone to the country, and I'd made up the beds with rugs, it really looked quite cosy.

The blitz by that time was hotting up, and as I didn't fancy tramping through the streets with shrapnel falling all round me, I spent many a night sleeping at the Post. It was really a good thing I did, for when the men were out on duty, it was useful to have some-one there to make tea or heat up soup when they came in for a few minutes, exhausted from their heavy work, which grew heavier and heavier as time went on, until they were all nearly at the end of their tether. My Birdie got very thin and haggard-looking, and the slight limp he'd always had since he lost his leg in the First World War, became much more noticeable. The others sometimes used to beg him to spare himself a little, for he was the oldest of them, but he never would. He insisted upon leading his party when they went out on a job, as they called it, and drove himself unceasingly, until one night he had a collapse when he returned with the others from an incident, and when he came to, it was to find himself on a camp bed in the basement shelter, with Mr. Benyon standing by with a dose of brandy and me dabbing his forehead with eau de cologne. He looked ruefully up at us and Mr. Benyon said firmly:

'Now, Chief, you're to lie here and get a night's rest and let us look after you. You've been driving yourself for weeks on precious little food and hardly any sleep, and if you don't look out you'll have a real break-down and we shall lose you.'

Birdie scowled and tried to raise himself in bed, then he gave an exclamation of annoyance.

'What's happened to my peg-leg?' he demanded.

'That's me,' said Mr. Crump, grinning. 'I took it away to stop you moving. Be sensible, Chief. The show's over for tonight—the bastards cleared off ten minutes ago and the All

Clear's gone. There's nothing for you to do, so you just lie still and try to get a little sleep. Any clearing up there is still to do, we can manage without you.'

'Well, if things have really quietened down. I will try to sleep a little—I *am* pretty well all in. I shall be all right after—after—'

His voice trailed off, and he was asleep, as instantly and completely as any baby.

'He'll be all right now,' I said to the men who were standing looking down at him. 'He'll sleep like a log, and I'll look after him. I've got the kettle boiling upstairs if you'd like a cup of tea or something before you go out.'

'Not now,' said Mr. Crump. 'We'll get you to make it for us when we get back, Skivvy. So long! Come on, Benyon.'

They clattered up the stairs to the ground floor and I drew up a chair to the bedside and sat down, savouring to the full this moment—the moment when I could, in truth, feel myself my son's mother. My Birdie! For a little while mine alone. He was so deeply asleep that I dared, actually, to lift the hand that lay on the rug that covered him and bring it to my lips, so softly that he never stirred. Then I laid it on my lap, cradled between my two hands, a brown, veined hand, strong and muscular, the hand of a man. And

I remembered the tiny baby hand that had curled round my finger long ago, and a kind of passionate ecstasy shook me as I looked at it and thought—'It is mine! All mine.' I had made him, I had borne him, I had given him up, and for years we had been parted, but now we were together once more. And as I sat there, watching over him, I made a vow that somehow, in some way, I would see to it that we were never parted again. No matter in what humble capacity it was, I would serve him until death severed us.

Almost as I made the vow, I heard a dull, but ominous thud, the sound of a muffled explosion, and the walls of the house that sheltered us trembled. I rose to my feet, listening. Surely the raiders hadn't returned? There had been no siren warning. Putting my Birdie's hand gently back on the rug I went over to the oilstove and turned it out for safety's sake, and then returned to the bedside. The sound came again, nearer this time—a dreadful sinister sound, followed by a roar, and the terrible familiar cracking and rending, the noise of masonry falling. The ground under my feet shook and shuddered and I saw that the wall beyond the bed on which my Birdie was lying was cracking and tilting inwards, while the great beam that ran across the ceiling from side to side, the main joist, was cracking and bending too.

And just below lay Birdie, still sleeping the sleep of exhaustion, despite the noise. There was no time to wake him—and anyway, he could not have moved quickly enough without his artificial leg. There was only one thing to do—and I did it. Just as the beam fell I threw myself across my son. There was a fearful roar of falling masonry. Then the beam struck me square across the back—and I knew no more.

*   *   *

Afterwards, when I was well enough to be told, I learnt that the explosions had come from a couple of bombs that had landed a few houses away without exploding, and then, a few hours later, had gone off one after the other, probably set off by people digging into the ruins to try to rescue some of their things. Fortunately the building we were in didn't entirely collapse. Only half the beam and a part of the side wall had fallen upon us, and the rescuers had found us, unconscious but alive, underneath a heap of rubble, with the beam lying across me. We were brought out comparatively easily, and Birdie was safe, except for bruises and shock. But my spine was broken, and they had to tell me that I should never walk again. Oddly enough, the only thing that really worried me when they told me was how I was going to earn my living if I were permanently in a wheel-chair. But I soon found that I had no need to worry about that. As soon as I was well enough to leave the hospital, Lord and Lady Stilwell had me brought down to the Dower House and given a lovely, ground floor room. There I was installed with all my little treasures around me, and they told me that it was to be my home for as long as I lived. They arranged for a little maid from the village to come in every day to see to my needs, and told me that they were going to look after me and I need never worry about anything any more.

It was, Lady Stilwell said with tears in her eyes, the least they could do, since I had made myself a cripple in saving Lord Stilwell's life. I smiled at that, thinking it was a small price to pay for the reward I had got—the right to live for the rest of my life in close touch with my Birdie, and to know that, as I had given him life at his birth, so I had given it to him again by saving him from death. Even though it had cost me a broken back, it was a price worth paying!

And so now for more than a year I have lived within sight of the Manor House, the house where my boy was born and where I gave him up to a woman who could give him so much more than ever I could have done. The war, thank God, is over, and I am much happier than I deserve to be. I know that. After all, I killed Tilda—and I'm still not sorry I did. If I hadn't, my boy wouldn't be where he is to-day. I've done a lot of dreadfully wrong things, I know. I had my baby out of wedlock, and I lived with a man I wasn't married to for years, and I murdered Tilda. But I think that God must have a kind heart for sinners, or He wouldn't have let me end my days in this blessed peace and comfort. My Birdie comes to visit me quite often, and sits and smokes his pipe and we talk of old times in the Warden's post, and sometimes he brings me a bunch of roses or a box of sweets or a magazine which he thinks might amuse me. Sometimes he brings his son, Master Evelyn, with him, and it twists my heart to see him—he is so like his father as a growing lad. Lady Stilwell comes, too, she rarely misses a week, and everybody is as kind as kind. I know in my bones that I shan't live much longer, and in many ways I shall be sorry to leave them all. But lately I've started to dream about my little Monsieur, who, I know, is waiting for me, and it was because of these dreams that I decided to try and finish this record of my life, for he was always so keen that I should.

And now it is done—and as I look at the pile of scribbled sheets I wonder if anybody will ever read it, and, if they do, what they will think of this Skivvy whose life story they have been reading. I must hide it somewhere though now, for I wouldn't have it found and read during my boy's lifetime for anything in the world. It would be safe in the old window-seat, I think, for the Dower House is seldom used now, and when I am gone, Lord and Lady Stilwell aren't likely to come to the old place. I'll tie it all up in the old grey gown I kept because Monsieur liked it. And when my little maid has gone out for her afternoon walk, I'll wheel my chair over to the window, and try if I can raise one of the sections and slip the bundle inside.

When that is done, I shall have nothing left to do but wait for the end—which I pray will come quietly and without pain. And when it comes may God, who understands mothers, grant that my Birdie may be at my side.

EPILOGUE

By Sallie Stilwell

EVELYN LOOKED across at me when, sitting before the fire in our bedroom, we had sorted out the last pages and come to the end of Skivvy's story.

'Well!' he said, drawing a deep breath. 'And where do we go from here? Do you think it's a true story—or has the old girl just been drawing upon her imagination and inventing a Victorian melodrama?'

'It *rings* true,' I said doubtfully. 'And she's got so much of the detail right, names, and bits of your family history, and, of course, we know that she's absolutely accurate as to what happened in the Warden's post.' Eve's mother had once told us the full story about that, and it tallied in every respect with Skivvy's account of it.

'*My* family!' said Eve with emphasis. 'Do you realize Sallie, that if this story is true, it isn't my family at all? I'm just the grandson of a tweeny-maid and a butler!'

I nodded. I had realized that all right, long ago.

'But not only *their* grandson,' I told him. 'You've got your mother's blood in you, too—the blood of goodness only knows how many dukes on her side.'

Eve laughed at that.

'Yes—and goodness, Sal! What would she feel like, with her mania for ancestors and pedigrees and all that, if she ever guessed the truth—that my father wasn't a Stilwell at all, but just the son of a "skivvy," as she calls herself?'

I nodded again. I was fond of my mother-in-law, but I knew her intense pride in her ancient lineage, the way she clung to the customs and traditions and all the rest of the things that belong to the old aristocracy. Nonsense, of course, when you come down to real values, but it all mattered tremendously to Mamma. She had always wanted Eve to marry into an English titled family, and she had found it hard to forgive him for marrying me, socially a complete outsider. Just a hick from Little Rock, Arkansas, who won a beauty competition and came to England to study elocution because she wanted to be an actress! Eve and I met at a party one night and we fell for each other at once—but remembering how long it took to persuade mamma-in-law to swallow the daughter of a man who kept a grocery-store as her son's wife, I realized what a mortal blow it would be to her pride if she knew the truth about her husband's birth.

After we'd got to be real friends, Ma-in-law and I, as of course we did in time, especially after our baby Tony came along, she used to tell me long stories of the pride and courage of the old families, and how much ancient lineage counted in producing people fine and fit enough to rule the masses. 'Blood will tell, Sallie, every time,' she used to say, and I hadn't the heart to tell her what lowdown skunks some of the scions of old families were—I came across some when I was beauty-queening, and I know! She was so happy and proud of the blue blood in her own and the family she'd married into, that I simply hadn't the heart to disillusion her. So I said:

'Whatever happens, Eve, we must never let her know. It's stupid, of course, because whoever your grandmother may have been you're still *you*. And, as a matter of fact I rather like your real grandmother, Skivvy—that is, if her story's true.'

'So do I,' said Eve. 'But Sal, it isn't only keeping it from Mother. If Skivvy's story is true, I'm sailing under false colours. I've no right to the title or the estates or anything else. I'm not a Stilwell at all—not even a Valentine! I'm a Skeffington! What on earth ought I to do about it?'

'Nothing at the moment,' said I firmly. 'You're not keeping anyone else out of the property.' That was true, the branch of the family that would have inherited if the Lord Stilwell of Emily Skeffington's girlhood had died without an heir, had become extinct in the First World War. 'It would be wicked to do anything while your mother is alive. Afterwards—well let's cross that fence when we come to it.'

Eve agreed with me that we simply couldn't do anything at the moment, not even send Skivvy's story to the publishing firm of our literary friend. I typed it out neatly and we put it away in a drawer in our London flat, both of us glad to postpone discussion of the ethics of the situation for awhile. Whatever one may think about titles—and being an American born and bred I don't think much—to discard one when you've got it isn't nearly as easy as it sounds, especially when, as in this case, there is so much dirty linen to be washed.

But I thought a lot about Skivvy in the months that followed, and so did Eve, and one day when we were staying at the Dower House, we tackled Mamma about her—not mentioning the manuscript, of course, but saying that we had been digging about in the window-seat and had unearthed an old dress which Eve thought had belonged to an old crippled woman who had lived at the Dower House when he was a boy, and whose name he thought was Skivvy. We showed her the dress, and, in the end, it was she who finished off Skivvy's story.

'Poor old Skivvy!' she said. 'She was a grand old woman. She saved your father's life, you know, Evelyn, in the blitz, when she was working at the Warden's Post with him. She threw herself across the bed where he was sleeping when the crash came, and took the weight of the broken beam across her back.'

Eve glanced at me.

'Damned plucky of her, he said. 'Wasn't she very fond of Dad? I seem to remember everyone saying that she was.'

'She was devoted to him,' said Mamma. 'She had worked at the Manor as a young girl and seems to have had quite a lot to do with him, though she wasn't actually his Nanny, though she rather liked people to think that she was. But certainly she thought the world of him, and God knows I was thankful for her devotion, since it saved his life. We did everything we could for her, the best doctors, everything. If it had been possible to operate and give her back her walking power, we would have had the best surgeons and felt it was worth whatever we had to pay. But the fracture was too serious, and she was too old, and there was nothing to be done but to make her as comfortable as we could for the rest of her life.'

'You gave her a happy end, anyway, I should think,' said Eve. 'I was taken to see her once or twice, I remember, and she always seemed cheerful enough. You used to go quite a lot, didn't you?'

'Oh, yes! I never missed a week. But it was your father she used to look for. Her eyes and her whole face used to light up the moment he came into her room.'

'How long did she live after you brought her down here?' asked Eve.

'About eighteen months. She just faded slowly out, and died, I am sure, without pain. Your father saw a lot of her the last week or two of her life. He had grown very fond of her, quite apart from his gratitude to her and his admiration of her courage in all that ghastly bombing. Towards the end, her mind began to weaken a little. Freddie told me that more than once as he sat beside her holding her hand, she used to stroke it and murmur something about a bird. I suppose she must have had a pet bird once. Freddie was there when she died. There were tears in his eyes when he came back and told me she'd gone.'

'How did she die? Tell us,' I said softly, for Mamma had fallen silent, and she roused herself to finish her story.

'There isn't much to tell, really. She had been half-dozing and he had been sitting beside her holding her hand, when suddenly she opened her eyes and said quite clearly; "I'm going now—and I know God's forgiven me because you're here." And with that she gave a little sigh and died.'

She paused again. Then, after a few moments she went on:

'We gave her a fine funeral and all the village came to it, though only a few of them could have known her when she was young. It was only two years later that your father died, and you don't need any telling as to what happened after that. Death duties and inflation and all the rest. And now the Manor House is a school full of noisy brats, and we're reduced to living in the Dower House.'

Eve got up and gave his mother a hug.

'Never mind, mother,' he said. 'We might

be much worse off than we are. Personally I love the Dower House, and I know that Sallie does, too. It's much more of a home than the Manor ever was. And now I think it's about time you went to your bed. There's a good programme on T.V. for you to watch to-night.'

She said good-night to me, and Eve took her up to her bedroom. He was gone some time, and when he came down again, he was carrying a portfolio under his arm.

'Prepare for the surprise of your life!' he said as he came into the drawing-room. 'What do you think Mother's just given me? She said that as we were interested in Skivvy we might like to see a collection of drawings she left. They were decorating the walls of her room, and after she died, they were shoved away in one of the attics. She'd told Dad she'd like him to have them as she'd no relations to leave them to, but Mother didn't care for them much, so they were just bundled up and put away. She told me if I liked to have them, get them down and show them to you, I could. So here they are.'

He dumped the heavy portfolio on the hearthrug, and threw it open, and inside I saw that there were two smallish canvases, and some sheets of thin board—the sort of board artists used for sketching. Eve handed me first the boards, and I found that they were covered with sketches—powerful, incisive drawings that even I who know about as much of drawing as a cow knows of talking Chinese, could see that they were brilliant. They were sketches of trees, animals, people—two market women talking, a small boy crying over a broken toy, a man in a ragged scarf playing a flute. But the greatest number were of a woman—of the woman we had grown to know so well, Skivvy.

Some were casual outlines, some more careful studies—sometimes they were of the feet and hands only, or of a naked torso. But mostly they were heads—and when Eve showed me the canvases, there she was again, in oils this time. Two portraits, one a head, the other a complete figure in the nude. How he must have loved his 'Emmee,' this little Frenchman who had pictured her so brilliantly! And, indeed, she must have been pretty then—though perhaps pretty is not quite the word. Piquant, attractive is better. The head was just a head and shoulders, the face half in profile, the shoulders showing the grey dress buttoned high to the throat, that we knew so well. But when Eve held up the second canvas, I couldn't help exclaiming in admiration.

It was obviously the painting called *After the Bath*, and it showed the model sitting naked on a bed, tucking up her hair in a towel to dry it. We could see now how beautiful a body she must have had, our Skivvy. Small, and rounded and dimpled, and exquisitely proportioned—a perfect Boucher type, Eve said, a dream-come-true for an artist to paint. And when one looked from it to the painting of the head, and saw the frank dark eyes and the curving generous mouth, one could well understand why Monsieur loved his Emmee so well.

Together we studied the two canvases, which were signed 'Jacques Yvetôt,' and the sheets of drawings. And at last Eve sat back on his heels—he had been kneeling on the hearthrug—and sighed with satisfaction.

'D'you realize what these are worth, Sal?' he said, and when I shook my head, he went on:

'As so often happens with artists, poor little Yvetôt was as poor as a church mouse while he lived. But after his death, his work came into its own, and since the War the prices of his pictures, especially his portraits, have soared! These are worth money. A lot of money. I'm going to take them up to London and show them to a dealer I know. Unless I miss my guess, the result will solve our worst worry—Tony's education.'

They did more than that. The sale of the pictures and sketches enabled us to buy a new car, move into a better flat, and left a nice sum over to invest. I made one stipulation, though. One of the drawings of Skivvy's head was to be kept, to use as a jacket and frontis-piece for her life-story when the book came out, and afterwards to be framed and hung in our flat. I felt in a queer way that she had taken us under her wing, and that to keep *one* portrait of her was the least that we could do.

Needless to say, Eve agreed to that. Darling Mamma died soon after she'd told us the end of Skivvy's story. She had been ailing for a long time, and we had been warned that her heart was in a bad state, so that we were not surprised when she slipped away quietly one night in her sleep. Our sorrow was mitigated by the thought that she died quite ignorant of Eve's true descent. I really don't know what she would have done had she ever got to know of the secret we had uncovered. After her death, Eve had a long talk with me as to what we should do about our discovery. Of course, being a Briton, he wanted to do the noble thing and publish the whole story to the world. I had the devil of a job with him! This British integrity may be very fine, but it's a damn nuisance at times, and I had to do a lot of hard talking before I got him to see sense. As I pointed out, it wasn't as though he was keeping a rightful heir out of his inheritance. There wasn't a rightful heir! Eve was the last of the line, and as for the estates—what with taxation and death duties, there were hardly any left worth counting. Just the Manor House, which was now a school, and the Dower House, and a handful of fields and old cottages. Besides, Eve was well-known now in the broadcasting and television worlds, and his title went over big with listeners and viewers. 'Mr. Skeffington' wouldn't be in the same street, and to change to that now, might be fatal to his career.

So after a lot of talkee-talkee, Eve agreed to let poor little Skivvy's deception go on; and I turned with enthusiasm to see about publishing her book. It was taken by the first publisher we sent it to, and—as though the gods couldn't do enough for us now that the tide had at last turned—an American firm snapped up the film rights. So it seems, one way and another, that our years of living from hand to mouth are over.

We used a pseudonym of course, and

altered the names of the people and places so that no-one should guess who were the characters in Skivvy's story. And, since everybody seems to take it for granted that it *is* only a story, it seems improbable that anyone will ever know.

Tony is growing up fast, and he has a younger brother and a sister, too, for, thanks to Skivvy, we could well afford to have them now. We have the London flat, and the Dower House is our country home. The Manor House is still a school, and a very successful one, and we get on very well with the headmistress—although we did have just a small spot of bother with her last year. She wanted the shrubbery of laurels and rhododendrons grubbed up to make more room for the playing-grounds, and she seemed quite hurt when we refused our consent. She couldn't understand why we did. It was old and overgrown and a lot of it was dead, anyway. It would improve the place so much if it went. But all Eve would agree to was to have it trimmed and pruned and some of the dead wood cut away, which didn't satisfy her at all—but Eve wouldn't budge.

'Some day, when Tony's taken over,' he said to me, 'he may choose to dig it up. I can't prevent that. But, at least during my lifetime, the rightful heir to the Stilwell name and fortune shall rest where Skivvy laid him—in peace.'